"In one minute we'll know."

Sam stood to the side of her to watch the next change, and Vicki closed her eyes, her heart hammering in her throat. "I can't look. Tell me when it's over."

A few seconds later, Sam huffed out a sigh. "Well. There it is," he said.

"Well? What does it say?" Vicki asked, still afraid to open her eyes.

"I don't know whether you'll be disappointed, angry, excited, or what," Sam said, and placed a hand on her shoulder.

"What are you?" she asked.

"I'm…pleased."

And he was. She could hear it in his voice. The softness, the love, the warmth. She opened her eyes and looked.

Positive.

Dear Reader

What a thrill to be a part of the 100th year celebration for Mills & Boon! They have provided great reading to many people for many years, and to be included is a thrill of a lifetime for me. Thank you for making all of this possible. Without the readers there would be no one to write for. Happy reading for many years to come!

Thank you for reading THE NURSE'S LITTLE MIRACLE. I hope you enjoy my second book for Mills & Boon.

Molly Evans

THE NURSE'S LITTLE MIRACLE

BY
MOLLY EVANS

MILLS & BOON
Pure reading pleasure™

All the characters in this book have no existence outside the imagination of the author, and have no relation whatsoever to anyone bearing the same name or names. They are not even distantly inspired by any individual known or unknown to the author, and all the incidents are pure invention.

® and TM are trademarks owned and used by the trademark owner and/or its licensee. Trademarks marked with ® are registered with the United Kingdom Patent Office and/or the Office for Harmonisation in the Internal Market and in other countries.

First published in Great Britain 2008
Large Print edition 2008
Harlequin Mills & Boon Limited,
Eton House, 18-24 Paradise Road,
Richmond, Surrey TW9 1SR

ISBN: 978 0 263 19979 6

Set in Times Roman 17¼ on 22 pt.
17-0908-39498

Printed and bound in Great Britain
by Antony Rowe Ltd, Chippenham, Wiltshire

Molly Evans has worked as a nurse from the age of nineteen. She's worked in small rural hospitals, the Indian Health Service, and large research facilities all over the United States. After spending eight years as a Traveling Nurse, she settled down to write in her favourite place, Albuquerque, NM. Within days she met her husband, and has been there ever since. With twenty-two years of nursing experience, she's got a lot of material to use in her writing. She lives in the high desert with her family, three chameleons, two dogs, and a passion for quilting in whatever spare time she has. Visit Molly at: www.mollyevans.com

Recent titles by the same author:

THE SURGEON'S MARRIAGE PROPOSAL

This book is dedicated to my friend and fellow writer Robin Perini. Thank you to Robin for suggesting that I write medicals in the first place! Your help and support is more valuable than you can ever know.
Molly

CHAPTER ONE

I'M AN idiot, camp nurse Vicki Walker thought as she drove through central Maine among pine forests, away from the city. Why, oh, why had she let herself be talked into this job? She knew why. She was an idiot!

With a heavy sigh she tried not to let her emotions overwhelm her and accepted her situation as temporary. Gil, the camp administrator, had begged her, and she had given in, even though her soon-to-be-ex-husband was the camp physician. From the minute she'd agreed three days ago, she'd known she would regret it. There was no way out of it now, so she'd just make the best of it.

Going back on her word to the camp wasn't an option. She'd just have to suffer through two months of hell in her personal life to help some needy kids. That was the bottom line. She'd agreed to help the kids, that's all.

Just ahead a weather-aged wooden sign pointed the familiar way to Camp Wild Pines, the rustic facility where she'd spent many summers as a camp nurse. Five more miles. The thought of seeing Sam again, working with him, and living in the same small infirmary, made her tremble. Sam always had had that power. But no longer. She wasn't the same woman that he had married. She was stronger, and she intended to prove it.

After settling into the infirmary, Dr Sam Walker waited for Vicki while busying himself with setting up the medical supplies in the small infirmary. He ran a hand over his face in frustration. Of all the damned luck. Just when he was starting to get used to the idea of divorce, Vicki gets dropped into his lap again. If they survived the summer without one of them walking out, it would be a miracle. How they were going to work peacefully in this small infirmary space was beyond him. When they had been happily married, the rough log building had seemed cozy, quaint, even romantic. Nothing about the rustic setting, the pines, the fresh air now seemed romantic in the least. Now it felt too close, too intimate, filled with memories he wanted to forget.

Tires crunching on the gravel outside distracted Sam. Vicki pulled up to the infirmary door in her red Mustang convertible. He'd bought it for her birthday last year, knowing he'd neglected her due to the extreme demands of his job as a pediatric intensivist, hoping it would make up for…something. He was surprised she hadn't sold it yet to get rid of any reminder of him. Then he smiled. She loved that car.

Vicki caught her breath as Sam descended the steps of the little cottage with a screened-in porch. The building was a welcome sight, but he wasn't. She hadn't seen him in months, and hadn't expected to see him the very second she pulled into camp. A little breather would have been nice, but obviously not meant to be, just as she and Sam weren't.

The emotions of the last year came flooding back, and her lips pressed together as nausea cramped her stomach, reminding her of the familiar ache of her past. For her own good she had to leave him. They just weren't good together any more. She'd realized it. It was time he did, too.

Staying married to a man whose job was more important than his family was something she could no longer do. Over the years he'd changed—less emotion, more control, less the man she had married and more doctor. She'd thought he loved her enough, but apparently not. She needed to be needed, but Sam needed no one. Not even her or their relationship.

This temporary excursion to camp meant nothing. Nothing had changed between them. The camp for underprivileged children needed her. Sam didn't. He'd made that abundantly clear over the last months. She cleared her throat, trying to choke down the emotions that threatened to spill out.

Pasting a smile on her face, she got out of the car with what she knew was a fake upbeat attitude, but she had to try, didn't she? "Hi, Sam," she said, and walked past him into the infirmary. Memories assaulted her from every side, making her gasp for air. Memories she'd struggled to forget, struggled to erase. Taking a few deep breaths, she tried to stay calm, tried not to let anything get to her. At least, not yet.

The screen door slammed as Sam entered with one of her suitcases. "Made it OK?" he asked, obviously uncomfortable with seeing her again as he shifted the bag from one hand to the other.

"Yeah," she said. Maybe he was regretting this situation as much as she was. But the kids always came first with him. Always had, always would. That much about him would never change. Children and patients were more important to Sam than she had ever been. After coming to that realization, the rest had been a no-brainer. Leaving Sam had been the only option left.

"I have to say I was quite surprised when Gil told me you were coming."

"I was pretty surprised he asked me, considering our…situation. How's the other nurse, do you know?"

"Recovering. The accident was pretty bad. She'll be in rehab for a few months, learning how to walk again."

Vicki huffed out a breath. In the face of that situation, her issues seemed petty. "Wow. I had hoped she'd be improved enough to take over in a few weeks, but it sounds like that's out of the question." Disappointment slumped her shoulders, but she was determined to get through this summer. Somehow.

"Pretty much."

Sam jingled the change in one pocket, the sound an irritating distraction, but he always did that when he was nervous. Taking a deep breath, she tried to focus, tried not to allow her limbs to quake the way they wanted to. "H-how have you been?" she asked, irritated that her voice cracked. They were just making small talk, but she felt as if she didn't know him any more. And he certainly didn't know her as she'd thought he had, or he would have known she'd needed him, would have known how devastated she'd been by his absences. They'd lived in the same house. How could he not have known, for God's sake? Tears pricked her eyes, but she blinked them away, determined to be stronger than ever. She had to be or she wouldn't be who she needed to be.

Sam's gaze raked over sleek blonde hair, the blunt ends now just brushing her collar. "You cut your hair."

Vicki glanced away from him, smoothing a hand over her hair, not yet accustomed to its recently cropped length. It was unexplainable, but it was something she had needed to do. Cutting her hair symbolized severing her old life, going on to something new. "Yeah, well, it was time to give up the long hair and grow up."

"It looks nice. Suits you." Sam's gaze raked over her. "You're looking well."

"Thanks. You, too." Vicki returned to the car for more suitcases, and Sam followed.

"Let me give you a hand," Sam said, and hefted a duffel bag. Once inside he dumped it at her bedroom door. "What do you have in there, bricks?" he asked.

"Shoes. You know I… Never mind," Vicki said, and turned away. "If you don't want to help me, fine. I'll do it myself." Unzipping one of her cases, she prepared to unpack and hoped he'd take the hint and leave her alone. He'd left her alone plenty of times in the last months. Why did he now decide to be this close? "It's been a long drive, I'm tired, and I want to get settled before the kids get here." Helping out at the camp was her only reason for being here, she had to remember that. As soon as her obligation ended, she was gone. That was her focus now. If she kept to it, she'd survive.

"I'll leave you now, if that's what you want."

"You left me a long time ago, Sam. I'm just making it final, so we can move on. It's that simple." Another handful of clothing into the next drawer up, and she pushed the empty suitcase beneath the bed.

"What are you talking about? You walked out on me, remember?"

"You never came home! Not for a week after I miscarried the last time." She'd never forgive him either. Never.

Sam took a deep breath, visibly trying to control himself. Vicki unzipped her other suitcase. Holding a handful of shirts, she opened another drawer and another until she had them filled. When she got to the top drawer, she paused. A small wrapped package lay inside. Vicki reached in and pulled it out, handed it to Sam.

"I'm not accepting any presents." No way, no how. She couldn't be bought, no matter how expensive the gift. It wasn't going to happen.

"Don't get too excited, princess. Just open it." The sideways smile on Sam's face almost made her want to open it. "No, I won't. This is not acceptable. Presents are not part of the divorce process." They were way beyond presents now.

"It was actually for the nurse who was supposed to come, but you can use it, too." He shrugged and looked away. "If you don't use it, give it to someone who will."

Puzzled, she opened the wrapping and frowned. "Bug spray?"

"Yep. The mosquitoes will eat you alive this year." Without another word, he left. Vicki set the bottle on the nightstand and shoved socks into the drawer. Quietly, she closed the door and leaned against it, then slid to the floor. The knot that had begun when she had agreed to this fiasco was growing. Her lungs burned with the need to breathe. How in God's name were they going to get through the summer without hurting each other more than they already had? There was too much hurt, too much pain locked in her soul to ever forgive Sam. But somehow she had to survive the next eight weeks with him.

Way too early the next morning something licked her ear and nuzzled her neck, urging her awake. Vicki stirred in the midst of a dream, immediately assaulted by the worst dog breath on the planet. Pushing the creature away, she sat upright. A white, curly-haired, four-legged beast masquerading as a dog had crawled onto her bed.

"Ugh! How did you get in here?" Vicki tried to shove it away, but the little dog was firmly entrenched.

Sam stopped in the doorway, watching as she petted his dog. "Now, Charlie, mind your manners. Sit," he said. The dog scooted back and sat on the floor. "Introduce yourself before you stick your tongue in her ear," Sam said. "Shake."

Charlie held up one paw. Vicki took it in her hand, then yelped as Charlie lunged forward to lick her face again.

With a snap of his fingers and a command of "Out" from Sam, Charlie dashed out the back door.

"When did you get him?" Vicki asked, wiping the slimy wetness from her face.

"A couple of months ago. I needed someone to keep me company at night who didn't want to know where our relationship was heading." Sam glanced away from her. "Breakfast is in the lodge in half an hour," he said, and left the infirmary.

Emotions pummeled Sam. The sight of her in bed would once have filled him with desire. Mornings spent snuggling together, cuddled up in the nest of their bed, were long gone. Too many months and too many harsh words had passed between them.

Mindless as to where he roamed, Sam's footsteps took him to the edge of the lake. Everywhere he looked, everywhere he turned were memories of his past life with Vicki. The lake and the countless times swimming or boating with her every summer. The fire pit and camp fires with her tucked against his side. The lodge, the hiking trails, everything hammered him with endless reminders, endless visions, an endless movie of his life, with Vicki in the starring role.

When Gil had told him Vicki would be the substitute nurse, Sam had almost strangled the man. Having Vicki in his life day after day as their marriage came to a close was more than he could bear. At least, that's what he had thought. But now, seeing her, living and working with her, was going to be harder than he had ever imagined.

Apparently sensing his mood shift, Charlie nosed Sam's leg. "Yeah, I know, boy. Bummer of a summer, eh?" He ruffled the dog's fur. "Let's go for a run." Hoping the physical activity would distract him from his tortured thoughts, he broke into a warm-up pace with Charlie beside him. But after forty-five minutes of exertion, Charlie was worn out and Sam was no closer to ridding his mind or his heart of Vicki. Walking to cool off, Sam was unable to turn off his mind.

Theirs should have been a perfect marriage. What could have been better suited to a physician than a nurse who understood the complications of the life of an MD? What should have been the perfect arrangement in Sam's mind hadn't turned out that way. He hadn't realized how much maintenance a successful marriage actually required. When they had been dating, their relationship had seemed to easy, almost effortless, and she had taken it in her stride when he had been called away, no matter the circumstances.

What had happened? With no answers, Sam entered the lodge for some breakfast.

After a hot shower and a protein-filled breakfast, Vicki wandered the grounds of the twenty-five-acre camp and revisited friends and familiar places. The two-story lodge made of oak and pine hadn't changed in years. Maybe a new coat of polish on the wooden floors, but the building central to life at Camp Wild Pines was the same.

While wandering down along the edge of the lake, a woman about Vicki's age approached, and gave a glad cry of recognition. Vicki found herself engulfed in a familiar embrace smelling of suntan lotion. "Ginny! How are you?" she asked as she hugged the swim coach.

"Great, just great." Ginny pulled back with a sad smile and sympathetic eyes to look at Vicki. "But I hear all is not well with you."

Vicki dropped her gaze away and looked out at the glassy surface of the water, unprepared for the power of the emotions burning through her. "No. Not so well this year." Though she tried to stop it, her bottom lip trembled, and her breathing came in short gasps. After a few seconds, she controlled the impulse to throw herself into Ginny's arms and have a good cry. Having suffered her own marriage loss, Ginny would understand her pain.

"Well, I'm here if you need to talk. The door's always open." Ginny gave Vicki another quick squeeze.

"Thanks. I'll probably be down here, bending your ear, before long." The impulse to give in passed, and Vicki could breathe again.

"When you're ready, I'll put the kettle on, and we'll have a good girl chat," Ginny said. "You know there is always chocolate in my cabin."

Vicki gave a small laugh. Every year Ginny had a canister full of chocolates for anyone who passed by. "I may need it before too long."

The phone in Ginny's office rang, and she

sprinted off to answer it, waving goodbye to Vicki as she left.

Strolling down to the edge of the water, Vicki kicked off her purple flowered sandals. With her feet in the edge of the cool lake, she stood for a few minutes, savoring the silken feel of the water tickling her ankles. So many times over the last few years this lake had brought her comfort and soothed the rough edges of her mind whenever she'd needed it. She hoped it would still be able to offer the same this summer because she needed its peace more than ever. With a sigh, Vicki retrieved her sandals and walked barefoot back to the infirmary.

At noon six buses crammed with children between the ages of seven and sixteen roared past the infirmary. She narrowed her eyes, wondering where Sam was. They had to get the preliminary exams started as soon as the kids got off the buses. Few of these kids had regular health care, so the camp provided a thorough physical at the beginning of the summer. Over the years Sam and Vicki had caught a few serious illness in the early stages and got treatment for the children.

Sam entered the infirmary seconds before the first camper did.

"Where have you been?" she asked, unable to hide the displeasure of her tone.

"Taking care of business," he said. "Let's get on with it."

By the end of the day, she and Sam had examined 175 throats and twice as many ears. They had inspected as many eyes for conjunctivitis, a highly contagious infection that could run rampant in a group of kids in such tight quarters, but thankfully found none.

One small boy, underweight for his age of eight, lingered by the door, his brown eyes looking too large in his thin face.

"Hi," Vicki said, and motioned for him to come forward, her heart aching for the shyness she saw in him. "Do you need to see the doctor again?" She stooped so she could be closer to his height, and held out her hand to him. Hesitantly, with a quick glance at her, he took her hand, the small bones noticeable in her grasp as he entered the main room of the infirmary.

He kept his gaze to the floor. "No. I just wanna pet the dog," he whispered, then glanced again at Vicki, hope and fear glimmering in his eyes. "Can I pet him? I won't get in the way. I'll be quiet, I promise."

"Sure you can. He won't hurt you, and you're not in the way at all." Vicki suppressed the urge to cuddle the boy against her. She called to Charlie, who crawled across the floor and pushed his wet nose into the boy's hand.

A grin lit up the boy's face, and his excited eyes flashed at Vicki. "He likes me! He really likes me."

"He sure does. His name is Charlie," Vicki said, her heart breaking for the boy, who obviously loved dogs. "What's yours?"

"Jimmy," he said absently, having now lowered himself to the floor and lain full length beside Charlie.

"Jimmy, you probably shouldn't lie on the floor—it's really dirty," Vicki said, thinking of all of the germs that collected on floors, as well as the dust and dirt tromped in by all of the kids. She hadn't had a chance to sweep up after the bunch of them had moved on.

Jimmy jumped up, his eyes wide with fright, his breathing rapid. "I'm sorry. I didn't mean to. I won't do it again."

"It's OK," Sam interrupted, and patted Jimmy's tiny shoulder, throwing a frown at

Vicki. "You can get dirty if you want to. It won't hurt anything."

Eyes downcast, Jimmy pulled away from Sam's touch. "My dad says I'm filthy, too." In a flash he turned and bolted for the door, leaving Vicki and Sam staring after him.

"What do you think that was about?" Vicki asked, not liking the immediate impression she was getting of Jimmy's family. Something wasn't right, but she didn't know what.

"These kids come from some pretty tough situations."

Vicki looked up at Sam, her eyes wide. "I know that, and I don't appreciate the glare."

"What glare?" he asked as he glared down at her.

She pointed at his face. "That one. Don't undermine my authority in front of the kids."

"Your authority?"

"Yes. You always intervene in things that are

none of your business. Like you don't trust me to handle a situation without you there to save the day." Had it always been like this?

"I don't—"

"Help," a voice cried, as three girls staggered through the doors of the infirmary. "I'm dying," the one in the middle said, and burst into tears. Blood flowed down the knees of both legs.

"We'll finish this later," Sam said, and scooped the girl up and set her on the examination table.

CHAPTER TWO

VICKI grabbed a dressing supply kit and a bottle of saline as Sam snapped on a pair of exam gloves. Now was not the time to get into it with Sam.

"What happened, girls?" he asked, then visibly cringed as all three chimed in at once.

"She fell."

"That dork pushed me!"

"We don't really know."

"Whoa. One at time, please, so Dr Sam can take a look at your knees," Vicki said, trying to keep the atmosphere calm and not feed into the hysteria of the girls. "What's your name?"

she asked the girl on the table, and placed an absorbent pad beneath her knees.

"Emily." Her blue eyes welled with tears as she looked at her knees.

"So, Emily," Sam said, as he held out a wad of gauze to Vicki. She poured saline over the gauze, and he dabbed at the blood, trying to see what was beneath it. "Why do you have blood dripping down your knees on the first day of summer camp?"

"Somebody pushed me, and I fell in the rocks." Though bravely trying to control her lower lip, it quivered anyway. "Ow, that hurts," she said, and tried to pull away. "Ouch."

"I have to clean out the wound so we can see if you need stitches," Sam said, and held onto her leg.

"Stitches? Oh, I'm gonna puke. I'll be ruined for life," she cried, and burst into theatrical tears.

The other two girls started screeching with

her, and Vicki interrupted before things got out of hand. "Girls," she whispered conspiratorially, and herded them to the side. "This is a very delicate procedure, and Dr Sam needs absolute quiet." She glanced over her shoulder at Emily on the table as Sam continued his exam. "If you can be quiet, you can stay with Emily, otherwise you'll have to wait on the porch. Emily needs you to be calm. Think you can do it?"

The wide-eyed girls nodded and remained amazingly silent. They each held one of Emily's hands, leaving Vicki free to assist Sam.

"Now then, Dr Sam, what else do you need?" Vicki asked as she returned.

"An irrigation syringe with saline. We need to get the gravel out so the wounds heal without any infection," he said, not even glancing at her. When there was a patient on the table, he was all doctor. Though determined to be professional in front of the patient, Vicki wanted to cram his irrigation syringe somewhere uncomfortable.

Together, Vicki and Sam tended to Emily's knees, removing embedded debris that could impair the healing process then applying steri-strips and a light dressing.

"Emily," Sam said, "you've been very brave, as have your assistants." After disposing of his gloves and washing his hands, he pulled out a prescription pad. With a flourish, he scribbled something on it.

"I need medicine?" Emily asked as her eyes welled again.

"Yes. A serious one." He tore off the page and handed it to her.

She read it, then grinned. "Ice cream? I get ice cream?" she asked, and smiled, her impish face lighting up as she looked at her friends.

Vicki had to smile at Emily's transformation.

Sam certainly knew how to get a girl what she wanted. Except for her. Then she sobered, reeling her thoughts back to the present situation. This situation had nothing to do with her. This was professional. They were working together for the summer, that was it. When the last bus pulled out of camp, she was going to be right behind it.

"You and your brave assistants get some ice cream on me. Take that to the lodge. Tell Bear to send me the bill."

The girls helped Emily down from the exam table.

"Come in every morning after breakfast so I can check your dressings," Vicki said, trying to keep her focus on the present, not wallow in the past.

"I will," Emily replied, as her friends helped her outside. The screen door slammed shut behind them.

Vicki avoided looking at Sam as she cleaned up the mess. She stopped and stared at the pink streaks of blood on the gauze. Blood… There had always been so much blood. And the pain had been horrible. Nausea rolled across her and she pressed a hand to her flat abdomen.

"Vicki?" Sam's voice and his hand on her shoulder made her jump. "Do you need some help?"

"What?" She blinked several times, remembering where she was. "Oh. I need to clean this up, don't I?" Grabbing the trash can, she started scooping the used supplies into it.

"Wait. Let me help you." Sam reached for the discarded dressing container.

"No. You shouldn't have to clean up this kind of stuff. You're the doctor, and I'm the nurse. It's my job to clean up the mess I've made." Yes, just remember the drill and everything will be fine. Just fine.

Sam's hands on her shoulders stilled her. "Vicki, look at me."

"No. Can't do that." She shook her head. If she looked into his eyes right now, she'd shatter. If she looked at him, she wouldn't be able to do her job. If she looked at him, she'd cry and never stop.

"It's going to be OK," he said, his voice soft and full of understanding that hadn't been there months ago. He pulled her to stand upright.

Tears filled her eyes as she thought of the dreams that had died along with their babies. Even with modern technology and all the available healthcare, she couldn't have babies. It seemed like all Sam had to do was look at her and she got pregnant. But no matter how hard she tried, she just couldn't make her body hold onto the fetus. Some women had baby-making bodies, and some didn't. She had the desire, but not the body to accomplish their dreams. The dream of motherhood was one she'd carried since she had been a child herself. And now that dream was dead. She had to move on.

"Do you want to talk about it? Did the blood remind you of…something?"

"I don't want to talk about it. Not now." She sniffed and wiped at her eyes, but he always knew when she was upset. That's what had once made him a great husband. He'd known when to love her, when to push her, and when to give her space. But in the end he'd given her too much space and not enough love, losing her in the process.

"It's a normal reaction—" Sam started.

"How would you know?" Pivoting away from him with barely controlled rage, she gave in. "How dare you assume to know anything about my reaction? You were never there to help pick up the pieces." If he'd only been there for her, their lives would be completely different now.

"You wouldn't let me be there with you, remember? I tried to help, but you pushed me away every time." Sam raked a hand through his hair.

"I needed you, and you went to work," she whispered. How more wrong could they have been for each other? How could she not have known that when they'd started out? Closing her eyes, Vicki shut him out, just as he had shut her out for so long.

She had to resist him. She wasn't prepared to get emotional with Sam again. But just then he touched her. Just rested his hands on her shoulders and pulled her back against his chest. Nothing sexual, nothing demanding, just an intimate, comforting gesture that she couldn't allow herself to indulge in or she would fracture into a thousand useless pieces. They were getting divorced, for heaven's sake. Letting him touch her was out of the question.

She moved away from him and immediately mourned the loss of his touch. At one time she had drawn great comfort from the circle of his arms around her. But now they were just an empty reminder of what she could never again have.

"Please, don't," she whispered.

"Don't what? Don't touch you? Don't comfort you when you are obviously hurting?" Sam turned away. "Dammit, Vicki. What happened to us? Above everything else we were always friends. Always. Now we don't even have that."

"How am I supposed to be friends with someone I can't trust to be there for me?" She huffed out a breath, trying to gain control over her emotions. "It's over, Sam. We can't go back. We can't go back to what we had."

Vicki walked down the hall to her room and closed the door, shutting him out, just as she had shut him out for months.

Guilt and anger warred within him. Part of him wanted to charge down the hall and have it out with her. But another part knew it was over, and she was right. As she'd said, he'd left her long ago. Sam closed his eyes. He hadn't meant to. How could he call himself a man, the way he'd behaved? So many times he'd watched his father ignore his mother. So many times she'd cried herself to sleep, thinking that Sam and his brother hadn't heard her.

But he'd known. He'd always known that some day he'd turn out just like the old man. Self-centered and distant, putting everything else before his family with the excuse that it was his job that provided for them.

Charlie nuzzled Sam's hand, distracting him. Sam sighed and leaned down to pet Charlie, and some of his frustration dissolved. He'd never been prone to angry moods, but over the last year or two with the demands of his job and the problems in his marriage, his temper had gotten worse and worse. He knew he'd hurt people, especially Vicki, but he hadn't known how to begin to apologize, so he'd pulled back until he had been too ashamed to do anything about it.

For this summer he just wanted to forget everything except what was right in front of him. The kids and the camp. That wasn't going to happen if he and Vicki argued every time they were in the same room. Right now he needed to let off some steam.

He strode out the door, with Charlie bounding along behind him. "Come on, boy. Let's go hit some home runs," he said.

Sam loaded the batting machine with baseballs. The kids used softballs for safety, but he needed the crack and snap of a wooden bat hitting a solid, hard ball to satisfy him. With a protective helmet on, Sam took the batting stance.

And missed the first three pitches, which didn't improve his disposition. His focus was so off right now he couldn't have hit a soccer ball had one come flying at him.

"What're you tryin' to kill?" Gil, the camp administrator, asked from behind the protective netting.

"Nothing," Sam said, and swung at the next automatic pitch. And missed again. He dropped the bat and turned to Gil with a curse. "OK. What's wrong with this picture?"

"You've got it set too high. Lemme come in and set it right for you, then you can start hitting them out of the park." Gil entered the back of the batting cage just as the next ball was released.

"Sam!" he cried.

"What—?" Sam turned. Unable to avoid it, Sam took the ball in the chest and crashed to the ground.

"Sam!" Gil hurried over to him. "Are you OK?"

Sam coughed and clutched his hand over his heart. "Man, that hurts."

"See? I told you it was set too high. Should have hit you in the gut," Gil said with a grin, and helped Sam to his feet. "Lemme fix it before it puts the next one between your eyes."

Sam and Gil spent two hours smacking balls and talking about life. Although talking to Gil didn't really accomplish anything, it certainly helped get rid of some frustration. And it was more constructive than sitting around feeling sorry for himself. He'd never been self-indulgent, and he certainly wasn't going to start now, just because his wife was leaving him and his life was falling apart.

What he needed was a plan. He'd always had a plan as far back as he could remember. Vicki had thrown him a wild pitch, and he wasn't sure what to do about it. Divorce had never been part of his previous life plan. But, then, the miscarriages hadn't been part of that plan either.

Damn, he should have been there to hold her, comfort her and mourn with her, not leave her alone as he had. It had been some misguided sense of male protection that had backfired. Instead of protecting Vicki from his grief, he'd torn her apart, and he didn't know how to begin to fix it.

He returned to the infirmary and drank three glasses of water in the kitchen, then filled a plastic glove with ice and applied to it his bruised chest. That should decrease the bruising and ease the pain of the baseball injury.

He was reclining on the porch when Vicki

found him, fast asleep on the lounger with a half-melted ice pack dampening his shirt.

Puzzled, she picked it up. Unfortunately for Sam, the glove leaked frigid water all over him before she could pull it away.

He launched himself from the lounger. "What are you doing?"

"Nothing," she said, trying to hold back the inappropriate giggle that threatened. There hadn't been many times she'd gotten the jump on Sam. "The bag was melting, and I was trying to keep you from being dripped on."

"Thanks," he said, and whipped off his soaked shirt.

Vicki gaped at his chest. "Sam! What happened?" She stepped closer and reached out toward the dark purple bruise over his heart, but refrained from touching him. He was no longer hers to comfort or touch. She had to remember that.

"I took a baseball in the chest. It's nothing," he said, and turned away from her with a shrug. Male pride forbade him from telling her how much it hurt.

"You wanted to know what happened to us? That's what." Finally she had the courage to say it out loud. This was the last time he'd turn away from her with a casual shrug.

"What are you talking about?"

"You turned away from me. You've been doing it for years now." Figuratively and literally. Emotionally as well.

"I did not." He stiffened at the accusation and took a step away from her.

"Yes, you did. Every time something went wrong at the hospital, you went. It didn't matter if we had plans, dinner on the table, or I was losing a baby. You turned your back on me every time I needed you!" She almost choked on the anger pulsing in her chest. How could he be so sensitive to the pain of others and not see hers?

"Dammit, Vicki. I thought you understood."

"Understood what? That I came second with you every time?" Was it really that simple for him and she'd simply not seen it?

"I thought you understood how important my job is to me."

"I did. I do. I just didn't understand that it was more important than your family." How could anything be more important than that? Once they'd wanted a big family, but now she was grateful they hadn't had children. It made leaving him a little simpler.

"It's not… I didn't…" He sputtered to a halt.

Vicki took a step back from him. "Think about that for a while."

"*All campers and staff to the lodge. All campers and staff to the lodge.*" Gil's voice came over the intercom.

Sam sighed at the interruption.

"I don't think I'm going to go. I'll just stay here," Vicki said. She couldn't sit beside Sam and pretend everything was fine.

"C'mon," Sam said, his eyes sad. "I think we can both use the break."

CHAPTER THREE

DESPITE her initial misgivings, Vicki enjoyed the gathering. College students with a variety of musical and dramatic talents came from all over the world to spend their summers with underprivileged kids.

The musical performance had everyone tapping toes and clapping in rhythm to the familiar camp songs that tore at Vicki's heart. Vicki even smiled for the longest time she could remember in months. Closing her eyes, she tried to suppress the bitter-sweet memories of summers here with Sam, the pleasure they had taken in helping kids while planning their own family. Now that their dreams and their marriage had shattered, Vicki realized she needed something else to fill the void in her life. Work wasn't enough.

At the end of the gathering, kids scattered to settle into their cabins, get to know their bunk mates and the counselors with whom they would spend the rest of the summer.

After dinner she returned to the infirmary and met Charlie waiting outside the door. "What are you doing here? Sent to spy on me?" Charlie wagged his tail and gave a charming whine that she found irresistible. She scratched him on the head and let him inside. "The kids ought to be here any minute," Vicki said.

When the group of children requiring evening medications arrived, Charlie approached each child gently, sniffed every one, and seemed to memorize their scent. By the end of the short after-dinner clinic, every child had scratched Charlie's ears or rubbed his belly and gone away feeling better. Vicki could see why Sam had taken an instant liking to him. The little rag-mop dog was already wagging his way into her heart.

Sam hadn't returned after dinner, which was for the best, she supposed. The more time they spent apart, the less time they would spend arguing. She went to bed and read until she was too tired to dream.

A loud banging on her bedroom door woke Vicki during the night, and she yanked it open, her heart already racing. Without having to ask, she knew instantly what was happening. The high-pitched wheezing of the boy, held tight in his counselor's arms, announced a severe asthma attack.

"Sam!" Vicki cried as she took Jimmy from

the counselor and carried him to the exam table. "Sam, I need you!" With trembling fingers, she opened the oxygen tank and hooked a mask to it.

Charlie barked at Sam's door, and then Sam was there beside her, his presence calming her fears. Facing a life-threatening situation alone under the best of circumstances frazzled her nerves. Here, alone at camp, she would have been a mess without Sam's presence beside her. He specialized in respiratory emergencies and, despite their personal problems, she trusted his clinical judgment and skills implicitly.

Vicki strapped the mask over Jimmy's wide-eyed face, hoping his lungs weren't too constricted yet to utilize the oxygen. "Breathe into the mask and try to slow down." She spoke in a quiet tone, trying to calm the boy as well as herself. "You're with us. You're going to be OK."

Sam grabbed a stethoscope and listened to Jimmy's back. "He's really tight. Get a neb set up," he said, and held the mask, though Jimmy tried to claw it off. Air hunger, that desperate need to breathe, sometimes caused panic and people tried to remove the one thing that was helping them. "Don't fight me, buddy. Don't fight. You use too much energy. Shh."

The soothing tones of Sam's voice rolled through her and she took a deep breath, letting his words work on her, too. He knew just what to do, what to say. As Sam held the boy and distracted him with a little rhyme, Vicki pulled more equipment and medication from the supply closet. With trembling fingers she snapped each piece of the nebulizer set-up together. "I'll hook it right to the mask so we don't have to take it off."

"Good idea," Sam said, and patted Jimmy's

back, soothing him. "Do you have asthma?" he asked.

Unable to speak, Jimmy nodded, his brown eyes huge in his small face.

"What's your name?" Vicki asked the counselor who paced back and forth beside them.

"Lester." He stopped and clenched his fists in front of him, his eyes as wide as Jimmy's. "How can you two be so calm? The kid can't breathe!" Lester gulped down a few ragged breaths.

"You can go back to the cabin if you need to, Lester. We'll take over from here. We have it under control," Sam said.

Vicki knew Sam was trying to give Lester a hint to calm down.

"OK," Lester said, and blew out a deep breath. "Sorry. I just lost it for a minute."

"You did the right thing by bringing him here immediately." She turned to Sam after checking the fluid level in the neb set-up.

"First treatment's almost done. Want a saline treatment, too?" They'd worked together long enough for her to anticipate his preference.

"Yes, let's do that. The saline mist will soothe his lungs and thin the secretions." Sam finished assessing Jimmy. "Are you allergic to anything? Did you eat anything weird at dinner or afterwards in your cabin?" Asthma attacks were often triggered by unknown, sometimes emotional factors, but foods and environmental allergens as well.

Jimmy shook his head. His breathing had started to ease, and he wasn't quite as wide-eyed and panic-stricken as he had been just minutes ago. A little shot of relief infused into Vicki.

This was what Sam was so good at. This was what he did. Did she have the right to ask him to give it up or take it from him? What if someone else needed him, too? Was she just being selfish?

"You're going to be OK," Vicki said, thankful they had gotten the situation under control so quickly. "Your lungs sound better already, so try to relax and let the medication work for you." Vicki rubbed his back as the aerosol treatment infused.

Again, he nodded. This time he tried to speak, but couldn't get enough air and just croaked.

"Don't talk right now. You can tell us all about it in a few minutes," she said, enormously relieved that he was responding so quickly to the treatment. Asthma ended the lives of countless children every year. When the lungs didn't respond to treatment, despite high-tech equipment and medication, the child suffocated from lack of oxygen. Vicki was glad that wasn't Jimmy's situation.

Charlie sat beside her foot and whined, wagged his tail and vied for attention until she looked down. "Sorry, Charlie. You can't help with this one," she said, but scratched his head anyway.

"Maybe he can," Sam said, and lifted the scruffy dog up with Jimmy.

"Sam! A dog doesn't belong on an exam table," Vicki protested, certain every germ and speck of dirt on the dog's body was about to be sucked into Jimmy's lungs.

"He's fine," Sam said, dismissing her concerns. "Jimmy has the mask on, and Charlie might help him feel better."

Very carefully, Charlie lay down with his head in Jimmy's lap. Focusing on the dog, Jimmy's wheezes eased in minutes. By the end of the second treatment he was no longer struggling to breathe and his heart rate had slowed to a normal range.

Sam listened to Jimmy again and gave a nod of satisfaction. "You sound great, Jimmy. Vick, let's check his saturation and see whether he needs to stay over with us or can return to his cabin."

Vicki clipped the monitor onto Jimmy's finger. "Ninety-seven percent. Very good."

"Now can you tell us what happened?" Sam asked, watching as Jimmy continued to stroke Charlie's head. The dog's golden eyes glazed over with pleasure.

"I got scared," he said, and shrugged, keeping his gaze on the dog.

"It's his first time at sleep-away camp," Lester said. "Problems at home," he added in a whisper to Vicki.

"You're well enough to go back to your cabin for the rest of the night," Vicki said, not agreeing with Sam's method of utilizing Charlie as a distraction, though certainly the results couldn't be argued with.

"Can Charlie come with me?" he asked, his eyes bright with hope.

"No, he has to stay with us here. Not everyone likes dogs as much as you do, but if Charlie makes you feel better, then you can stay with him in the ward room for the rest of the night," Sam said.

"Can I really?" he asked Vicki, all traces of his asthma gone as he removed the mask.

Vicki ruffled Jimmy's hair. She was glad to see him so lively. She hated respiratory emergencies for the powerlessness they made her feel. But with Sam there, problems magically faded away, the way her irritation evaporated now. Unfortunately, that skill hadn't translated to their personal relationship. "Sure. I'll just go make sure it's ready for you and put a blanket on the floor for Charlie."

"Cool!" Jimmy said, and kissed Charlie on the head.

Vicki swore the dog smiled.

CHAPTER FOUR

VICKI dragged herself out of bed later that morning just in time for clinic. She skipped breakfast in lieu of sleeping in for another much-needed forty-five minutes. After the late-night events with Jimmy, she needed a little more rest to handle the kids.

Emily and her ever present ladies in waiting held court for twenty minutes after clinic to ooh and ah over the progress of Emily's wound.

"This looks good. No infection, and you will probably just have a tiny scar on each leg," Vicki said, pleased the wound would heal without any trouble.

"Just a little scar?" Emily asked, sounding disappointed.

"Dr Sam did a good job," Vicki said with a quick laugh that faded as the screen door opened and in walked the man himself.

"What did I do good?"

"Fixed my knees!" Emily said, and her face turned bright red as Sam leaned over to inspect the wounds.

"Well done, if I do say so myself," he said, and winked at her. The other girls giggled and turned varying shades of pink.

"Let me put the dressings on and you can go," Vicki said, rolling her eyes at the reactions of the girls to Sam's presence. "If you feel feverish, come back at once."

Minutes later the girls were out the door, blushes and giggles following in their wake. Once upon a time she'd had that same reaction to Sam, so she could hardly blame them for their responses.

"How did clinic go?" Sam asked, watching as Vicki restocked the supplies she had used.

"Fine." She didn't look at him. She couldn't. Every time she did, she lost part of herself in him, which was something she could no longer afford.

"That's it? Just fine?"

"Yes. Nothing unusual." Did her fingers have to start to shake now? Couldn't she hold it together just a little longer? Maybe saying it aloud would help her to *feel* fine, not the mess of nerves she usually was. Fine was good. Fine was…fine. Maybe some day she'd be fine again.

"We need to talk, Vicki."

The vibrations of his voice chased memories down her spine. How could she go on all summer like this? Reacting to every word that came out of his mouth?

"We're talking right now." It was simple. Just open your mouth and say the words. Just like talking to any other person. There was nothing special about Sam. Really. Nothing special. Nothing at all.

"We're making small talk like we don't even know each other, and that's not the same," Sam said, and took a step closer to her, invading the barriers that she had put up with distance.

"We don't know each other. Not any more." As long as she denied it, it was true, wasn't it?

"We need to call a truce, even if it's just for the summer." Sam watched as emotions chased across Vicki's face. Her wide blue eyes were so expressive he could always tell her mood, but no more. The bright blue was covered with a mask of sorrow that he'd put there.

"A truce?"

"Yes." Sam took another step toward her. "If we don't put our issues aside, it's going to be a very long summer for everyone."

Could she do it? Could she set aside her needs once again for the good of the children she and Sam card for? Hadn't she done it enough already? Then she let out a deep sigh. Fighting with Sam the entire summer wasn't what she wanted either. Could she just go with the flow, as she'd once done? Setting aside her needs for the summer wouldn't hurt her. Would it?

"OK. It's a good idea. I'm glad you thought to bring it up." She nodded.

"Thank you," Sam said with a nod. "So how was the clinic this morning?"

Vicki shrugged and continued with the supplies. "OK. Just the usual morning meds."

"Thanks."

They fell into the routine of a doctor-nurse relationship. The steps were familiar as they'd taken this walk many times in the past. There was safety for both of them in pulling back into their roles, and they both knew it.

Somehow, some way Sam knew he had to let her go the way she wanted. If that was the only thing he could do to make up for the past, then he would.

The remainder of the day passed quickly as Vicki spent most of the time tucked away in the infirmary, reviewing charts, learning histories, and spending as much time away from Sam as possible.

As the evening clinic came to a close, Vicki noticed the unmistakable earthy fragrance of wood smoke in the air. She stepped outside to find the entire camp gathered around a huge bonfire. She hadn't been to a bonfire for years, not since she and Sam had dated... She mentally shook herself, not daring to tread on ground that she had covered over with concrete. Still, she smiled and returned briefly to her room for a jacket. Charlie followed her toward the gathering. She stood at the edge the group as the sun slid over the horizon. The brilliant orange and rust hues of the sunset were the perfect backdrop against the flames.

Someone played a guitar and led the kids in camp-fire songs, reminding her of her days in Girl Scouts and camping with her family. And summers past with Sam.

Watching the children reminded her once again that she was a failure. With no children to call her own, she'd failed in her life's dreams. She knew some people were happy without a family, but that wasn't what she wanted, what she needed. She wanted everything life had to offer and that included having children. But every miscarriage pushed her further from her dreams and without a supportive husband beside her, those dreams would never be fulfilled.

"Hi."

God, why did Sam always show up when she was at her most vulnerable? Did he have some sort of radar that tuned in to her emotions? Turning away as her lower lip trembled, she tried to wipe her eyes on the shoulder of her jacket. Sam's hand clasped the back of her neck gently and began to rub a slow rhythm that never failed to sooth her. But she knew it was wrong and took a half-step away from him, but he moved with her.

"This is supposed to be fun, but you're tense. What's going on?"

"Nothing." She stole a quick glance at him. It was a mistake.

Without a word, Sam pulled her against his side, and she let herself lean into him. For just this one moment in time she gave in and let him comfort her, let him hold her as she'd needed him to hold her months ago.

What had she done? It was essential she forget about the warmth, the strength of Sam's embrace and the need she had for it. Yet denying herself his touch was painful. Now that she'd given in again, how was she going to live without it?

"This reminds me of our days at the beach when we were dating," he said, and kissed the top of her head, just as he had then.

Just as he did it he pulled back, startled, and looked down at Vicki. "I'm sorry. I shouldn't have done that." Bringing her against him and kissing her had seemed so natural a motion that he'd forgotten for a moment they were no longer a couple. But now, staring down at her face so close to his, he no longer knew what was right. An overwhelming need to put the past behind them, to start over again, washed through him. This woman had been his partner, his life mate, his lover, and his best friend. He'd built a life with her, and now that it was ending, could he take the steps to rebuild the trust between them? Could he trust her not to hurt him again? Could he trust himself not to fall into old patterns? He didn't know and right now he didn't want to think about it.

Trembling with needs he didn't understand, he pulled Vicki closer. Even standing amidst a crowd of people he wanted to sink into her and kiss her as he had before their lives had become so complicated, so distant, so broken.

"Are you OK?" he asked, his voice rough.

She nodded. "Thanks. I'm tired, so I think I'll turn in early."

Sam watched her go and cold guilt filled the void she left. No, she was right. They were no longer compatible, no longer had the same dreams that they'd once had. They had to end it here, for both of their sakes.

Vicki was being suffocated, and she dragged herself from the depths of a claustrophobic dream. Charlie jumped up onto her bed, and she woke up fully with his urgent barks ringing in her ears. As soon as she opened her eyes, she knew the burning in them wasn't caused by lack of sleep but from a real fire. Smoke billowed through the infirmary, choking her as she breathed it in.

She leapt from the bed and clung to Charlie's collar as she crawled from her room. "Where's Sam?" she mumbled aloud, and Charlie whined and growled. "Find Sam, Charlie. Find Sam!"

Charlie would have leapt forward out of Vicki's grasp if she hadn't held fast to him. They inched along the hallway to where smoke billowed against Sam's closed door.

Vicki coughed and hammered on his door with one fist. "Sam, wake up! There's a fire! Sam!"

"What…?" Sam flung the door wide and inhaled smoke deep into his lungs. Vicki tugged at his sweatpants, and he dropped to his knees, coughing and hacking. "Hang onto me," Vicki cried, and felt him take a fistful of her nightshirt while he crouched, trying to clear the noxious fumes from his lungs.

"Out, Charlie. Out! Find the door." Vicki hoped the dog could lead them to safety.

With another whining bark Charlie led them to the nearest door, and they tumbled out onto the dew-covered grass. Coughing and gagging, they gasped for breath and endured enthusiastic kisses from Charlie. Vicki hugged him to her. "You're such a good dog! You get a big steak today," she promised.

Sudden, excited shouts from all over the camp interrupted the small celebration.

"Put a hold on that steak," Sam rasped. "We're not done yet."

Looking at the soccer field, Vicki gaped at the fire that was spreading quickly, licking its way through the dry grass and on to the edge of the woods surrounding the camp. On the other side of them small fires were dotted all over the grounds. So far no buildings were going up, but if they caught, all the children would be surrounded by fire with nowhere to go.

"Call 911," Sam tried to yell, but his voice was so hoarse only Vicki heard him.

"Where's the phone in the lodge?"

"Kitchen," he whispered, and stood up then clasped her hand, squeezing it, infusing his strength into her. "I'm going back to get equipment."

Vicki looked up at the smoldering roof of the infirmary. "You can't!" Terror filled her.

Sam pushed her toward the lodge. "Go!" Sam disappeared back inside.

CHAPTER FIVE

VICKI raced to the steps of the lodge. A shower of sparks burst from the top of a flaming pine as the hot pitch bubbling inside the tree exploded. Shielding her head with her hands, she jumped over the fallen branches and stumbled up the stairs, trying to avoid burning embers with her bare feet.

Strong hands helped her over the final step, and she looked up. "Bear!" The grizzled old cook held onto her. "Call for help. Call 911."

"Already done, girl. Come inside out of the smoke." With a heavy sigh Bear lumbered into the lodge. "Are you OK? Are the kids OK? Where's Sam?"

"He's gone back into the infirmary. Oh, my God, he's gone back in!" If something happened to Sam, she didn't know what she'd do. Even though they weren't together, she didn't want to see him hurt.

"He'll be fine, girl. Don't worry." Bear patted her on the back.

"I hope so," she said, unable to look away from the scene before her eyes, and her stomach clenched. Disaster was written all over the camp. Trees, buildings, and fields smoldered. Someone obviously hadn't put out the bonfire.

Kids and counselors raced in panic. Their emergency plan hadn't prepared anyone for this. The grassy field where they would usually convene was ablaze. The particularly hot summer hadn't been accounted for. Somehow she had to get everyone to come to the lodge. "Bear? Where's the intercom?"

"In my office," Bear said, and charged forward with Vicki right behind him.

Seconds later Vicki spoke over the system, hoping that it worked. "Attention campers and staff. Everyone, calm down or we're going to have injuries. Everyone, calm down." Watching from the window, she saw the chaos begin to slow down, but there was still no sign of Sam. First she had to help the kids. "Everyone, come to the lodge so we can account for all campers and staff. Everyone come to the lodge." Lines of campers and counselors emerged from the chaos and moved towards the lodge.

But she didn't see Sam or Charlie. Dammit, where were they? Though she worried for their safety, she had to get the kids taken care of first.

Sirens filled the air the flashing lights of firetrucks and emergency vehicles arrived at the camp in the pre-dawn light.

"Counselors, take a head count and keep your kids together."

Wails and cries settled down as everyone hurried in to the lodge where Vicki set up a hasty triage area. "I need someone to find Sam and help him bring equipment over here," she said.

"I'll go," said Rory, the soccer coach from Scotland.

He raced out of the lodge and returned with arms loaded with equipment. Though only a minute or two had passed since their dash from the infirmary, Vicki felt as if she had aged ten years. Worry turned to relief as she watched Sam enter the lodge, trailing behind Rory with the portable oxygen tanks and a backpack full of gear.

Heading straight toward her, she could see the concern in his eyes.

"Are you OK?" he asked her, his bloodshot eyes quickly assessing her condition.

"I'm fine." Without another thought she hugged him to her, needing to feel his heartbeat against her, even if it was for only a instant. "Are you OK? Did you breathe in smoke? Do you need oxygen?" So much damage could happen in just a few minutes.

"I'm really OK, Vicki. Don't worry."

With a nod, she tried to calm herself. "I've set up triage over here."

An agonized scream rent the air, and the hair on the back of Vicki's neck stood up. The savage cursing that followed gave her a hint that someone was hurt and not liking it at all.

A group of two counselors, with a third hanging by the arms between them, hurried toward Vicki and Sam. "What happened?" she asked as they set the counselor on the table.

Sam cranked up the oxygen and put a mask on the man's soot-covered face.

"Me mate," one of them said, and shoved a hand through his hair. "He was holding off the fire while the kids got out of the cabin. The whole bloomin' thing collapsed in on him." He cursed and clenched his hands into fists. "He fell right into the fire. I saw the whole damned thing."

"What's his name?" Vicki asked as she tried to cut off his clothing to assess his injuries. Looking around, she wondered if they could give him some privacy, but for the most part kids and counselors were busy elsewhere and not paying attention to the situation.

"Adam."

"Adam? Can you hear me?" she asked, and shone a light in his eyes, checking the pupil reflexes. "I need you to tell me where you hurt the most."

"Everywhere, dammit," he cried through the mask, his breath wheezing in and out through clenched teeth.

"Sam? Can we give him something to calm him down?" Vicki questioned, hoping they had enough supplies.

"Yes, of course. A few milligrams of morphine, I think, until he's taken to the hospital." Sam kept a hand on Adam's shoulder to keep him flat on the table. If he squirmed around, Vicki knew he risked injuring himself further, tearing already fragile skin.

"Let me start an IV, get some fluids going, too. Do you have the E-kit?" she asked, then located it on the floor beside them. "Oh, I've got it," she said, and pulled out a pack of pre-filled morphine syringes. "I've got anywhere between two and ten milligrams. What should we start with?"

"Go with four until we see how he tolerates it, then we can go up from there."

After being assured that Adam had no allergies, Vicki inserted an IV into the back of his hand, one of the few places that remained untouched by injuries, and administered the injection. "Adam, this will help you relax a little and take some of the pain away."

In minutes his breathing eased, and he closed his eyes in obvious relief. Without a word, Vicki and Sam went to work, stripping his clothing off and covering him with a sterile cloth moistened with sterile saline to prevent infection of his wounds.

"Sam, what do we do now?" Vicki asked. "I've no experience with burns."

"You're doing great, don't worry. We need to ship him to the burn unit in Portland. The little hospital here can't deal with his injuries."

"OK. OK," she said. The small bubble of

pleasure at his compliment eased some of her tension.

They sent him off in the ambulance to the local hospital, which would then transfer him to Portland via helicopter. If his injuries were as serious as they appeared, he had a long road ahead of him.

Before Sam and Vicki had a chance to catch a breath, the next patient appeared at the table.

Two hours later, after seeing about twenty kids and counselors for smoke inhalation and minor injuries, Bear brought a tray of coffee to them. Sam guzzled his black while Vicki added a bit of sugar and cream to hers. "Bear, you're a lifesaver," she said, and grabbed a donut, too. Without thinking, she picked a sugar-glazed one and handed it to Sam.

"What's the camp look like out there now?" Sam asked, tucking into the much-needed donut.

"It's a mess, though no buildings are totally

destroyed." Bear clicked his tongue and shook his head.

"At least that's something," Vicki said. She knew Bear had been at this camp for more years than she'd been alive. The devastation was obviously difficult for him.

"The soccer field's a loss and some of the woods are burnt, but Gil's been talking about clearing it for another soccer field anyway. Maybe we can do that now that the fire has given us a start." He nodded, seeming to come to a decision without any input from anyone else.

"What about the infirmary?" Vicki asked, and looked at Sam who had been inside it last.

"Just a few holes that can be patched. The roof didn't go up." Sam gave a lopsided grin. "You might have to get some new clothing and shoes if the smoke damaged them."

"I won't worry about that now," she said. "I wonder what set off the fire?"

"Somebody was supposed to sit with the fire until it was out," Bear said with a stern frown. "Damned kid fell asleep."

"I'm sure it was an accident. Nobody does something like this intentionally," Vicki said. But the damage to the camp was massive.

Jimmy came to the triage area as Bear departed.

"Are you doing OK?" Concerned about all the kids with asthma breathing in smoke, she brought Jimmy up onto the table. Sam listened to both lungs with a nod. "Sounds good to me," he said.

"I'm OK. I just came over to pet Charlie. Where is he?"

Sam and Vicki looked at each other.

"He was with you," Vicki said, as she realized she hadn't seen Charlie since she'd left the infirmary.

"No, he followed you to the lodge," Sam replied, and searched her eyes for answers.

"Oh, no," Vicki said. The concern she saw in Sam's eyes for the missing dog panicked her. She hoped nothing had happened to Charlie.

"That's OK, I'll pet him later," Jimmy said, oblivious to the concern of the adults.

"I need to find him, Vick," Sam said, and grasped her arms, urgency ringing in his voice.

Vicki's heart twisted, and she nodded. She wanted to help Sam, and she wanted to find Charlie. "He wouldn't leave camp, would he?"

"I don't know. The sirens and the chaos might have scared him. He was a pound puppy, so who knows what happened to him before I got him?" Sam's mouth compressed into a thin line.

"Go," Vicki said without hesitation. "I'll handle things here. Go find him. The kids are settling down now. We'll be fine."

Sam dashed into the infirmary and called for the dog, even looked under the beds and in the ward room, but he was not there. Back outside Sam staggered to a halt, taking in the devastation the fire had wrought so quickly. Bear had been generous when he'd said the fire gave a start on the new soccer field. Fire had consumed the forest for half a mile.

God, he hoped Charlie hadn't gone anywhere near it. Sam dragged a hand over his face in frustration, trying to think of all the possible scenarios. If Charlie had bolted with fear, there was no telling where he could be by now. Miles away. Or gone for good.

"Charlie!" Sam called. "Charlie!"

He waited, and walked around the cabins, down by the water and called for his dog. An answering whimper made Sam close his eyes in relief. "Charlie? Where are you?" Sam half crawled beneath the porch of a building and found Charlie hiding in the dark. "Come here, boy. It's OK now." Sam helped the shaken little dog come out from beneath the building.

When Vicki looked up again, Sam entered the lodge carrying Charlie, and she rushed over to them. "Oh, what happened?" she asked as she took in the dog's condition and the dirt covering Sam. "Poor guy. Where was he?"

"He was under the machine shed. He must have bolted through the woods," Sam said, his voice husky with emotion. "He's got burns everywhere from falling ash."

Charlie whined and licked Sam's face as children gathered around to offer sympathy. "It's OK, boy," Vicki said, enormously relieved that Sam had found him. She'd only known the dog a few days, but he'd already won her over. She knew what he meant to Sam and that was the more important issue. Sam's responsibility streak ran deep. But that's one of the things about him that had appealed to her. "You're gonna be good as new, and we'll get you that steak I promised." She knew the dog couldn't really understand her, but she felt better just saying the words.

While Sam held Charlie, the dog remained motionless, though his muscles trembled as Vicki cleaned his wounds and applied antibiotic ointment to the cuts and scrapes. "I hope this stuff is OK. What works for humans ought to work for dogs, shouldn't it?" She looked at Sam for confirmation, hoping she wasn't doing anything wrong.

"Thank you, Vicki."

"I didn't do anything. You found him." She looked away from Sam's eyes. The hurt in them was almost too much.

Sam grasped her wrist and held her until she looked into his soot-covered face. "I mean it. Thank you."

"You're welcome," she whispered as tears welled in her eyes. Some unnamed emotion simmered in her chest as she watched them. Sam cared very deeply, and she had always known that about him. If only he'd been there when *she* had needed him. Vicki had to look away from the tenderness and relief on Sam's face. Busying herself with little tasks, she stayed away from Sam until she was in control of her emotions again. A rock. That's what she needed to be when she was around Sam—a rock, impervious to his influence.

By mid-afternoon everyone in camp was exhausted. The fire department finally left after delivering their preliminary report to the Gil.

Sam wearily approached the camp administrator who looked very grim. "So, what's the word?"

"The word is *stupidity*," Gil said, and tossed the handwritten report across the picnic table to Sam. "We should have had a contingency plan for this but, dammit, I thought I had hired responsible staff." In frustration he pounded a fist on the table.

"You did, Gil, you did. But accidents happen, sometimes with devastating results." He scanned the report and shook his head. This was bad news for the camp, which seemed to hang by a financial thread every year anyway.

"I know, I know," the weary administrator conceded. "I'm trying to have patience, but the insurance premium hike is going to kill us. It could shut down the entire camp." Gil shook his head in disgust.

"It's a struggle every year, but somehow we make it. We'll make it through this crisis, too," Sam said. Somehow things always worked out.

"I'm just not prepared to go down without a fight," Gil said.

"Why don't you talk to the adjuster first? It shouldn't be an automatic rate hike, should it? Maybe you can cancel a bus trip to cover the cost or something." Sam wanted to think of anything to help the camp. These kids who came every year needed it. Hell, he needed it, too. Without this retreat to camp in the summer, his work life would drive him crazy.

"You're right, Sam, thanks." Gil smiled wearily and patted his mate on the shoulder. "We won't go down without a fight, I'll make sure of that. But first I have to call all the parents now. Could you give me a list of the children with injuries so I can report to their parents or guardians?"

"Sure. Let me talk with Vicki," Sam said with a nod, "but I believe there were just a few scrapes and bumps, no smoke inhalation and no burns among the children. Your counselors were very responsive and very responsible for their kids."

Gil nodded. "That's good to know." He shook Sam's hand and left the lodge for his office.

Sam approached Vicki. "Are you tired yet?"

Vicki raised a brow and looked down at the grubby nightgown she still wore. Sam's sweatpants were covered with small burn holes. "I think a shower and a nap would be really good about now."

"Come on, I'll walk you back," he said, and grabbed an armload of equipment to return to the infirmary. Vicki loaded her arms as well.

"I'm just glad there was only the one serious injury. This could have been catastrophic," Vicki said, as they walked slowly across the compound, Charlie hobbling along behind them.

"Gil's got a good staff and everyone apparently listened to the timely instructions over the intercom. That was a brilliant idea, Vick. I'm proud of you."

The glitter of admiration in his eyes made her heart blip unevenly for a moment. She looked away as a blush warmed her face and neck. A compliment from Sam meant something. Or it would have meant something a long time ago. Now she wasn't so sure. "Thanks. It seemed to be the best way of getting everyone's attention at once."

"You always were fast on your feet in an emergency."

"I wish I could apply that to other aspects of my life," she said. If she had thought things through, maybe she'd never have married Sam in the first place. But at the time she had been so in love with him, nothing could have stopped her.

"What do you mean?" Sam asked, and slowed as they approached the infirmary.

"Never mind. I shouldn't have said

anything." She opened the door and stepped inside, then held it for Sam and Charlie.

"No, it wasn't nothing. Freudian slips are there for a reason." Sam deposited his equipment on the floor and took Vicki by the shoulders, his hands gentle but unyielding. "Tell me what you meant. After all the time we've been together, you owe me an explanation for something."

Tears welled in Vicki's eyes as she stared at her almost-ex-husband. She'd known the most intimate parts of her life with his man. She'd given him her love and now she had to take it back. "Do you think giving up is easy for me?"

"It's not easy for me either. If you don't want to be married to me, fine. But, Vicki, you have to tell me why." His voice cracked slightly, the anger and despair that he'd kept in check for months bubbling over.

"Children are your life, Sam, and I can't give you any of your own."

"You can't be serious. The miscarriages were not your fault." Had he somehow made her think that she was to blame, as he'd made her think she was to blame for his self-absorption, when it was really his fault?

"But what if it is? What if there's something wrong with me, but the doctors can't find it? What if it's something I'm doing or something I'm exposed to that I don't know about? It's been three times that we've lost them, and I can't take it any more!"

"Vicki—"

"I'm a failure, Sam. At having children, at marriage—everything." Vicki jerked out of Sam's grip, and he let her go. For now. He'd never really heard her talk so painfully about the miscarriages before. He'd given her space and time to mourn them, as he had needed himself, but she hadn't healed. Now he wasn't sure if he had either. Some people never healed from such devastating losses. Clinically he knew that, but seeing Vicki suffer through it was painful. The last baby had been twenty weeks when it had died inside her. That was almost big enough to survive.

Now Sam knew that something in Vicki had died as well, and he was responsible for it. She put on a brave face to get through the day, smiling through her pain for the sake of the kids. But there was always that underlying sadness and grief that never went away. He'd also been so busy with his hospital practice that it had obviously escaped his notice until she hadn't been able to take it any more and had run.

Sam hung his head. How could he have been so blind? Maybe he was just as responsible for the break-up of their marriage as Vicki was. Living things that were neglected withered and died. That had happened to their marriage, but he didn't want it to happen to Vicki.

She was wrong. He was the failure, not her.

CHAPTER SIX

IN AN attempt to clear his mind of the day's events, Sam was about to hit the shower when Jimmy and Lester came in. "So what's going on with you two?" Sam asked, and lifted Jimmy up onto the exam table.

"Vicki asked me to bring Jimmy by after that asthma attack the other night to make sure he was still doing OK," Lester said.

"Good idea." Sam applied his stethoscope to Jimmy's back. After listening to all lung fields, he said, "You sound as good as new. If you have any trouble, just come back."

Jimmy jumped off the table. "Is Charlie here?"

"Yes, he's on the porch, resting. You can pet him if you'd like, but he has some injuries we need to be careful of." Sam's jaw clenched as he thought of the suffering Charlie had gone through because of him. Did he have to hurt everyone he loved? Was he incapable of having an honest, loving relationship with anyone? Even a dog?

"OK, I will. Did he get hurt in the fire?" Jimmy asked, and crouched beside Charlie.

"Yes. But he'll be fine in a few days," Sam said. "Dogs are good at bouncing back when they know someone loves them."

Vicki watched from the doorway as Sam knelt and assisted Jimmy to pet Charlie. Though Charlie didn't move much, he leaned back to accommodate a belly rub, making Vicki smile just a little.

"That's a good boy," Sam said, and lay down on the floor with Charlie and Jimmy.

With a deep breath and what she hoped was a genuine smile on her face, she stepped forward. "Hi, guys. What's going on here?"

"Charlie's hurt, so I was petting him to make him feel better," Jimmy said. "Dr Sam says dogs heal faster if they know they are loved."

Vicki's gaze cut to Sam, and she wondered if that sentiment translated to the human species as well. But she couldn't spend the entire summer feeling sorry for herself.

"I'm sure Dr Sam is right about that. Charlie looks better already." Vicki joined them on the floor of the porch and added her hands to Charlie's back.

"I guess it's time to head back to the bunkhouse," Lester said. "We've got a chess match going that we don't want to miss."

"But I don't know how to play chess," Jimmy said, getting up from the floor.

"That's OK. I'll teach you," Lester said as they headed out the door.

Vicki and Sam sat on the porch floor, flanking Charlie, who didn't know which way to turn for affection. He stuck his nose in Vicki's hand and gave Sam access to his belly.

"Is that true what you said to Jimmy? About dogs healing, I mean." Vicki kept her gaze on Charlie, unable to meet Sam's eyes.

"I think so. Most people heal faster if they have a support system around them. I figured dogs are the same."

"I see." A quick laugh escaped her throat, and she looked up at Sam, wishing he'd been there to support her. "Dogs aren't too far away from being human, are they?"

Sam smiled, but looked away from her. "Right. I like dogs better than most people I know."

Vicki sat with Sam, the silence between them almost as tangible as if they had touched. "I know Charlie means a lot to you. He's going to be OK."

Sam reached out to her and clasped her hand in his. With a quick tug on her hand he drew her to him and placed a warm kiss on her cheek.

The feel of Sam's skin against hers, his lips moving against her cheek, stilled her movements. Here was the gentle, loving Sam she'd fallen in love with. Where had he been for so long? Was he truly gone? Opening her eyes, she stared into Sam's face so close to her own, but resisted the urge to reach out to him. Something, some unnamed emotion, swam in his eyes. Had he felt it, too? That little sizzle of their past between them? With one lingering stroke of her palm along his face she pulled away from him. She could never go back.

"It's been a big day," she said. "I'm going to bed now."

Swam looked up and met her gaze. "Goodnight, Vick."

Sam stayed where she left him on the porch with Charlie.

Jerking awake, Vicki breathed heavily in the dark, trying to orient herself. "Wow," she said aloud, brushing sweaty hair back from her face. She threw off the damp sheet and stood, her body needing action to shake off the cobwebs of the disturbing dream. The past should stay where it was, not replay over and over in her dreams.

Curling her toes away from the cool floor, she stuck her feet into a pair of ancient sandals and padded to the kitchen for a drink. The stove light blinded her when she snapped it on. Pouring a small glass of milk and breaking out the graham crackers she settled at the little table. A slow tread alerted Vicki to Charlie's presence.

"Did I wake you, buddy?" she asked, and reached down to pet his head when he nuzzled her bare leg. Unable to resist, she broke off a cracker and gave a piece to Charlie. "It's not a steak, but you deserve a snack, too."

"He'll get fat if you keep that up," Sam said, and Vicki jumped. "Don't let him give you the poor-starving-dog routine. He's a mooch."

"You scared me," she said. "I didn't mean to wake you." The only peace she found sometimes was alone in the middle of the night.

"It was your shoes." Sam rubbed a hand over his face.

"My shoes?" Frowning, Vicki looked at the sandals.

"I remember hearing those shoes slap across the kitchen floor at night when you were worried about something. The sound was so familiar, it woke me."

"I hadn't realized." Had her late-night trips

to the kitchen had a pattern? Not that it mattered now.

"Are you OK?" Sam asked, as he settled at the table across from her.

Vicki dunked a cracker and ate it, thinking of how much to tell him, how much she wanted him to know. He wasn't supposed to be her confidant any longer, but there was no one else. "I don't know. Something woke me." She shrugged, trying to shake it off.

"What?"

"A dream." The dream had been about them, when they had been in love and in lust.

"Something you want to talk about?" Stifling a yawn, Sam focused on her.

Vicki couldn't remember the last time he had invited her to talk. Maybe he was changing. Maybe she was changing. "Not really. I'm OK."

"Sometimes dreams are the mind's way of

working out things we find difficult to face in the daytime."

"I know. But I don't think this was working anything out." A sigh tumbled out of her, and she resigned herself to telling him about it. "It was about us. When you proposed." Squirming in her seat, she looked at him. She hadn't meant to tell him, but tonight she had the confidence to say things out loud that she normally wouldn't have. Night had a way of dragging the secrets from her.

The grin that shot across Sam's face took years away. The lines of fatigue disappeared for just a second and made Vicki realize how tired he must be. The relief he had from work was never much—even at camp he never seemed to relax.

"I remember it." He nodded, but then the grin faded. "I remember it well. Those were good times, weren't they?" Sam sighed, as if giving in to his own memories of that time.

Somehow, sitting up late at night was easier than bearing his scrutiny in the full light of day. She could almost fool herself into believing they were married, having a late-night chat. Almost. But the pain between them was too much.

"If you want to talk, you know where I am," he said, and stood. He moved away, brushing her arm with a light touch, leaving her and Charlie alone.

She gave Charlie another cracker and listened to him crunch as she tried to figure out what to do. Being with Sam in such close quarters wasn't going to work. It was proving too easy to fall into their shared past, too easy to remember the good stuff, forget about the pain, and too easy to fall back from her goals. Maybe she could bunk with Ginny for the remainder of the summer.

No, that wouldn't work either. If someone

came to the infirmary in the middle of the night, she needed to be there, not indulging in her own self-pity. She'd just have to suck it up, put her big-girl act on, and deal with it.

Days passed with Sam and Vicki abiding by their truce, avoiding each other for the most part and working together when they had to. Vicki had organized the clinics after each meal and started getting to know some of the children who came daily for their medications.

Sam didn't come back to the infirmary until very late most nights, helping Gil prepare insurance claim forms. Charlie stayed with her most of the time, seeming to have adopted her since she had treated his wounds.

The second Saturday morning, Camp Wild Pines was the scene of an equestrian event. Anticipation hummed through the lodge at breakfast and hung on through the first clinic.

Some of the campers were going to perform in the show ring for the first time. Vicki got to the arena early to set up a first-aid table. Bear had set up refreshments and light snacks for the kids.

The first hour of events went well for all of the smallest children. Vicki should have been happy for the campers, but watching as each child finished their tasks and received their ribbons caused a tinge of despair to run through her. She would never have the opportunity to watch her own child perform at events like this. Another milestone in life that she would miss.

"What are you looking so glum about?" Sam asked, as he took a seat beside her.

"Why is it you have to sneak up on me all the time?" Dammit. He was getting annoying, showing up every time she had a moment of pain, unable to mull it over in private.

"I didn't sneak. You were deep in thought. What's up?"

"Nothing. Just watching the events." Crossing her arms over her chest, she stared at the arena. "I'm not talking to you."

"Vicki," Sam said, his voice deep and husky, drawing an unwanted response from her. "I thought we agreed to a truce."

"I can't do this, Sam. I thought I could, but I can't stay here with you all summer and not think about what I lost. I'm trying to make the best of this, but I need to grieve, too." Those babies had been her chance for a future, and she'd lost every one of them. With each loss she'd lost a piece of herself, and she was afraid she'd never get it back, never be whole again, never be able to move on.

"There is so much pain in you, I can feel it across the room. Talk to someone." He cleared his throat and looked away. "I understand that you can't talk to me, but I want you to know that if you want to talk, I'll listen." Meeting her gaze, he held it. "I've not been very good in the past but, I promise, this time I'll listen."

No. He wasn't going to turn her inside out again. Not now. She couldn't let him. "Sam—"

Screams filled the air, and she turned back to the arena. "Someone's down," Vicki said. Sam leapt to his feet and together they raced across the arena where a horse thrashed on its side.

"Get that horse up," Vicki cried, not knowing who was beneath it, but a child could be crushed in an instant by a horse.

"Where's the trainer? Get that horse up!" Sam yelled.

"I've got him!" One of the handlers grabbed the bridle and aided the horse to its feet. The child beneath the animal hadn't moved since Vicki and Sam arrived.

Hands shaking with fright, Vicki grasped the head of the child before the horse had gotten fully upright. "Emily!" Vicki cried. "Sam, get the immobilizer."

"Got it," Sam said, panting, and slipped the hard plastic neck brace onto Emily. "I hope she's just fainted," he said.

"There are no obvious limb breaks, but she could have hit her head. Even with the helmet on, she could have a head injury." Vicki hoped that Emily's condition wasn't that serious. But her first thoughts raced to the worst possible scenario.

"Check her pupils," Sam said, and listened to her lungs with a stethoscope. "No collapsed lungs. How are the eyes?"

"They're good." Vicki tossed the flashlight back into the E-kit, relieved Emily wasn't seriously injured. In the short time they'd been at camp, she'd grown attached to the little girl.

"She's probably just concussed. We'll need to send her to town for X-rays, though." Sam leaned back and took a deep breath. "This is all we can do for now."

"Sometimes the best isn't enough," Vicki said, determined to do everything to help this little girl. "We have to do something else. I'm going to start an IV." Dammit, she wasn't giving up on Emily yet.

"Go ahead and start an IV, but no fluids. I think she'll be fine, Vicki. Don't worry." Sam placed a hand on Vicki's arm and stilled her movements.

"Don't worry? How can you say that when her life might be fading right now?" Vicki pulled out an IV start kit, but Sam's hands prevented her from continuing and she was forced to look at him.

"Let go of me," Vicki said, and tried to move Sam's hand.

"No. You're overreacting."

Though Sam's voice was gentle, she didn't want to hear it. So what if he was right? So what if she was overreacting? She couldn't stand by while another baby died. "Get away from me," she said, struggling in Sam's grip. "I have to help her."

"We are helping her. If she does have swelling in her brain, we don't want to add fluid. Vicki, stop it right now." He shook her once.

"I can't!" God, she couldn't help herself. Hauling in deep breaths, she tried to calm down, tried to hear the sense in Sam's words, but she didn't want to.

Everything was coming back at once. The pain, the disappointment, the loneliness, and the failure. Her failure. "It's all my fault. Oh, God, it's all my fault."

"No, Emily's going to be fine."

Sam held Vicki against him. As she cried on

his shoulder the ambulance arrived and the paramedics took Emily off to the hospital.

Ginny approached Sam. "Do you need some help?"

"Thank you, but no. I've got her. This is my responsibility." The shame for which he would bear silently. "You can help keep an eye out for the kids, though."

"Sure." Ginny patted Vicki on the back. "I'll direct any emergencies your way, but I can handle the first-aid stuff."

"Thanks, Ginny." Sam led Vicki up the hill to the infirmary where they could have some privacy.

Once inside, Vicki pulled away from Sam. "Leave me alone."

"No. I've left you alone too much already." He had never realized the depth of her pain. But now it slapped him in the face. He'd failed her, big time.

"You left me alone plenty of times, and it never bothered you. Why do you care now?" Vicki paced back and forth across the little room.

"I'm sorry…"

"For what? Hurting me? Sorry my babies died? What?" She stared at him, her pain unmasked, her fury unleashed. And he deserved it.

"*Our* babies. They were *my* children, too. I haven't forgotten about them." Sudden fury overcame Sam at the wrongness of everything that had happened between them. "If I could take it all back, I would. The pain, the babies, everything, but I can't."

"I'm not perfect. I tried, Sam. I tried with everything in me to be perfect, but I'm not. I'm sorry." Her sobs, torn from the deepest part of her, washed through him. He didn't want to see it, didn't want to hear it, but he had to for Vicky's sake.

"I never asked you for perfect, Vicki, that was all you. How could I? I'm nowhere near perfect either." He took her by the shoulders and made her face him. "We were just two people struggling along, doing our best." It was all he could think of, all he had left.

"Was it really our best? Did we really try as hard as we could have?"

Covering her face with her hands, she tried to shield herself from him, but she couldn't disguise her pain. He felt the blame and despair that she felt. He deserved every bit of it.

"It wasn't fair. I hated that you went through the miscarriages, but wasn't your fault."

"Wasn't it? I'm the one who carried them, and *I* lost them. Me, not you." Tears poured down her face, and he wanted to brush each of them away if she would let him.

"I lost them, too."

"You don't know what it was like, Sam. Feeling that tiny life moving inside me, the fulfillment that I'd finally done something right in my life, and then having it ripped from me."

"I'm sorry, Vicki." Sam's eyes moistened. "It's not your fault," he whispered. "It's mine."

"Don't give me that rubbish. How could it be your fault?"

"I wasn't there when you needed me. Especially when you needed me. I wasn't there for you when I could have been."

"What do you mean, 'could have been'?" Vicki stopped, her attention riveted on him.

"I thought I was helping you." Unable to deny it any longer, he had to confess his feelings to her.

"What are you talking about? I needed you, and you went to work. It's that simple."

Sam sighed. "I didn't want to burden you with my grief. You had enough physical and mental stuff to work through. I didn't need to add to it." Confession was supposed to be good for the soul, but this did nothing except make him feel more like he'd failed her.

"What? I *needed* to feel your grief, Sam. Sharing it with me would have been kinder than walking away from me, letting me think you didn't care." She stared at him, unable to believe what she was hearing. "You let me think you didn't care, that losing our babies didn't matter to you."

"I'm sorry," he said. "I couldn't give you my grief. I'm a doctor, I'm supposed to fix things, make people better. What kind of doctor was I if I couldn't make my own wife better? Couldn't save my own child?"

Sam took a step closer to her, but she retreated. "Don't touch me." Right now she couldn't bear it. There was too much to think about, too much to process.

"I thought it was for the best at the time."

Vicki crumbled to the floor, her sobs tearing his insides to pieces. Sam knelt beside her and put his arms around her. "What I did was very wrong, and I'm sorry."

Vicki turned into him and wept. At least she let him hold her, touch her and comfort her, as he should have long ago.

CHAPTER SEVEN

NEEDING some private time after her blow-up with Sam, Vicki skipped dinner. Being emotionally fragile was getting old, and she needed some alone time to pull herself together. As she prepared for the evening clinic, Lester rushed Jimmy to the infirmary in respiratory distress.

Vicki heard the crowing sound of respiratory stridor before Lester opened the door. She kicked in to ICU nurse mode and her years of experience took over. "Put him on the table. What happened?" She opened the oxygen tank and placed a mask on Jimmy, taking in the bluish tinge to his lips and the wide-eyed fearful look. This wasn't good.

"I don't know. He had dinner and just started to breathe wrong," Lester said.

"Did he cough? Did he choke on his food? What?" Vicki tried to get a handle on what had happened and shone a flashlight down Jimmy's throat. A piece of food lodged in the esophagus could cause epiglottitis and the resulting crowing sound as air squeezed around the blockage. She couldn't see any foreign objects.

"No, nothing. Just ate his dinner as usual." Lester paced and his hands tore at his hair.

Sam raced through the door. "What's the situation?"

"Acute respiratory distress, but no choking, no food in his esophagus that I can see." Sam's arrival couldn't have been timed better.

"Nothing precipitated the attack?" Sam

asked Lester, and grabbed a stethoscope to listen to Jimmy's lungs.

Wide-eyed, Lester only shook his head and wrung his hands.

"Get the E-kit," Sam said to Vicki. "He's bad enough we may need to intubate him." Intubation was essential in such life-threatening situations.

"He's going out," Vicki said as Jimmy went limp in her arms. "Jimmy? Stay with me." She shook her head. "Sam…"

"Damn. Get the paralytic. Smallest ped dose you can get by with." Sam helped lay Jimmy on his back so Vicki could organize the medications.

"He weighs thirty-four kilos." Vicki administered the medications that would sedate Jimmy temporarily. "Meds in." Sam placed the endotracheal tube down the boy's throat with ease. Placing such a tiny tube between swollen vocal cords wasn't easy in a distressed patient.

Vicki picked up Jimmy's hand to place an IV in it and gasped. "He's got a rash. Look at this." Without waiting for Sam to inspect the weals erupting all over Jimmy's body, she turned to Lester. "Go get Bear and bring him back here right now. We have to know what was in that meal."

Lester raced out of the infirmary.

"I think it's anaphylaxis. He's got to be allergic to something from dinner." Vicki pressed her lips together as she slid the IV catheter into Jimmy's vein.

"Get the epi kit, give him a dose now." Sam attached oxygen to the tube now in Jimmy's lungs and gave him breaths, forcing in life-sustaining oxygen.

Vicki injected the proper dose of epinephrine into the IV line and hooked Jimmy to a monitor. "His rate is already high. One forty-nine."

"Kids can handle it. I'm more worried about his breathing right now. What's the saturation?" Sam looked over her shoulder at the monitor, his nearness a comfort as they worked together.

"Oxygen saturation is at eighty percent. Bag faster," she instructed, and Sam compressed the ambu-bag at a quicker pace.

Lester hurried into the infirmary with Bear behind him. "He's here. He's here."

"What was in tonight's dinner?" Vicki fired at him before the screen door slammed shut.

Bear ran down the list of foods served for dinner. Nothing jumped out at Vicki as a common source of allergens, but there had to be something in there that Jimmy had reacted to. Jimmy's breathing started to ease, and Vicki gave another small dose of sedation to keep him calm. They needed him quiet for just a while longer.

"We need to know more. I want to know exactly what was in each of those recipes. This kid has an allergy, and we've got to find it." Working to save Jimmy drew on strength she hadn't known she had. But this was what she did. What she and Sam did. They saved lives.

"You know I don't give out…" Bear started his automatic response, then looked at Jimmy. "Where's the phone?"

Minutes later Bear's assistant dashed across the compound with a binder stuffed with haphazard papers sticking out from all corners. "But, Bear, you don't give the recipes to anyone!" his assistant exclaimed, looking at the medical scene. "Oh."

"This is an emergency," Bear said gruffly, and placed the binder on the table. "They should be right on top," he mumbled.

Jimmy started squirming on the table and reaching toward his face. "He's bucking the tube already. Think we can take it out now?" Vicki asked Sam, hoping they could remove the tube and ease his distress. Most people didn't like the foreign object in their throats, even though it helped them.

"I think so. What's his saturation now?"

"Much better. Ninety-five percent." She knew now his brain wouldn't have any damage from lack of oxygen.

"OK. If he's strong enough to fight it, he's probably ready."

Vicki explained what they were going to do, and Jimmy stilled, his gaze never leaving Vicki's face. After the tube was out, he sat upright, a mask of humidified oxygen misting into his face. Though he was pale, he seemed to be pulling out of the distress he was in.

"I'm going to set up a series of plain saline

nebs for him to keep those lungs moist," Vicki said.

"Good idea."

Bear read off the list of ingredients and spices in each of the dishes served at dinner. He kept it up for four recipes, but halfway through the fifth, Vicki stopped him.

"Wait. Back up to the last one." That had to be it.

"Brown sugar?"

"No, the one before that." She was more sure than ever. It was a potent allergen for some people, killing many people every year.

"Oyster juice?" Bear asked, the expression on his face incredulous as he looked at Jimmy. "He's allergic to oyster juice?"

"That's got to be it. Lots of people are highly allergic to shellfish."

"Not in Maine!" Bear scoffed.

"Lots of people are allergic to shrimp and

clams, Bear. Sorry," Vicki said, certain she was right. She turned to Jimmy.

"Jimmy? Can you eat shrimp or clams?"

"Don't know," he rasped. "Never had 'em. My dad says they're too expensive for kids."

"Want to try some? I have a great recipe for clam chowder," Bear asked, already starting to stroke his beard with one hand and flip through the binder with the other one.

"Perhaps not today, Bear," Vicki said. "Jimmy's had enough culinary excitement for a while. Let's find out if he's allergic before you let him sample the chowder."

"Oh, yes, yes, yes," Bear said, disappointment obvious on his face.

"I'd love the recipe, though," Vicki said, as she patted Jimmy's back, relieved the treatments worked. Another day, another emergency.

Bear snapped the folder shut. "I don't give

out my recipes." He and his assistant returned to the kitchen.

Vicki laughed after they'd left and hugged Jimmy to her. "I'm so glad you're better. You gave us quite a scare, didn't he, Dr Sam?"

"Sure did," Sam said to Jimmy, but he kept his gaze on Vicki.

"Before the summer's over, I'm going to get that recipe out of Bear."

Sam laughed. "Good luck. I know clam chowder's your favorite, but we've been coming here for years, and no one has gotten a recipe out of him yet."

"I'm willing to take on that challenge," Vicki said, a gleam in her eyes. "Now, let's get Jimmy settled. He's going to have to stay with us tonight. I'll get my pillow and sleep in there with you so you're not lonely, OK?"

"Cool! It will be like a sleepover, won't it?"

he asked, failing to see that the entire summer was one long sleepover.

"Lester, can you bring back Jimmy's essentials to get through the night?" Vicki asked, and began to put away the supplies they had used.

"Oh, sure. Pajamas, toothbrush, toothpaste." Lester counted on his fingers as he listed the items. "Anything else?"

"Don't forget my computer game!" Jimmy called. "It's in my backpack under my bunk."

"OK. Back in a few minutes." Lester patted Jimmy on the back and headed out the door.

He returned shortly with the supplies, and Vicki assisted Jimmy to get ready for bed. The ceremony of using the bathroom, putting on pajamas, and brushing teeth was something Vicki had never thought much about. But now, helping Jimmy with these small bedtime tasks, she thought that if she'd had children, it would have been a regular routine. "Does your mom help you with this stuff at home?" she asked.

"No." Jimmy looked away from her gaze in the mirror and spat in the sink, then rinsed his mouth. "She died a long time ago."

"I'm sorry. Your father must help you, then." The sorrows this child had faced in his short life rivaled her own. But he seemed to go on as if nothing bothered him. Maybe she could take a lesson from him. Life went on no matter what else happened. Attitude was what made the difference. Hers had been pretty crummy for a long time.

Jimmy turned toward the ward room. "My dad's mean."

Vicki slowly followed, watching Jimmy's little shoulders hunch over, the way they had when he had first come to camp. "What does he do?"

After crawling into the bunk, Jimmy cuddled into the covers with his computer game clutched in his hands. "He used to hit me and my brother, but he doesn't any more."

"Did he get some help?" How anyone could harm a child was beyond her. Someone needed to look into this.

"No. The state took me and my brother from him. Now he can't see us." Jimmy rolled over, his back to Vicki.

"Oh, Jimmy. I'm so sorry. But maybe the change is for the best." Vicki dropped to her knees beside his bed, her heart aching for this little boy and the trouble he had known in his short life. Nothing she'd ever experienced even came close to this.

"That's why I got to come to camp. They didn't have any foster-parents for me and Eric yet."

"Where's Eric?" Vicki hoped he was somewhere safe and with a loving family until he and Jimmy could be reunited.

"He's at another camp. In Vermont, I think. It was last minute and they said they couldn't put us in the same place." After a large yawn, Jimmy closed his eyes.

"I see," Vicki said, and tucked the covers up around Jimmy's chin. She wondered if separating the boys was a strategy to keep them safe should their father try to recover them. If she and Sam had been able to have children, she would have protected them with her life. There was no doubt in her mind that Sam would have, too.

Perhaps things could have been different between them if they'd loved each other enough, if they'd made job sacrifices… They'd still be married, they'd still love each other, they'd make plans for the future. Adoption wasn't out of the question. At least it hadn't been when they had been together.

"How's it going?" Sam asked from the doorway.

An image of Sam checking in on their own child caught her by surprise. If only… "He's asleep," she said.

"Good. He needs it after the day he's had." Sam crouched beside her bed.

"I need it after the day I had, too." Vicki still couldn't believe the emotional ups and downs she'd had today.

"Are you OK?" The concern in Sam's eyes also surprised her.

"I will be. Thanks."

"I'm sorry if I upset you today."

"It's not your fault. I thought I was over the miscarriages, but I guess I'm not. It just takes time, right?" She hoped so. She didn't want to live in this emotional roller-coaster for the rest of her life.

"It will. Every day you'll get better. You're stronger than you know, or you wouldn't be here now." Sam stood and moved away. "Goodnight, Vicki."

Moving to the bunk beside Jimmy, she lay down and stroked Charlie's head. Though physically and mentally exhausted, she stared at the ceiling for a long time before sleep overtook her.

Sam didn't go to bed, but instead chose the porch swing for a while. So much had happened today that he couldn't sleep, couldn't calm his thoughts or control the trembling of his hands.

Keeping his secret from Vicki had taken everything he'd had at the time. He was a man. He was supposed to protect what was his, not neglect it, not forget his promise to her, to himself. Realizing there was more of his father in him than he'd ever known hurt. He'd worked hard for years to overcome his past and he'd forgotten about Vicki in the process.

Becoming obsessed with success and money hadn't paid off. That was exactly what his own father had done. And his mother had suffered greatly, as had he and his brother.

But he was responsible, he thought, and leaned his head back on the porch swing and let the memories take him. It was his fault. It was always his fault that things went bad. If he'd been more responsible, he'd have known that Derek had been in trouble. But having fun with his friends at the lake had been better than watching out for his baby brother.

The sun and the water had been what had mattered to him then. As soon as he'd gotten his driver's license he'd gone to the beach with his friends to celebrate. That had been his life. Dragging his little brother around hadn't been in his plans. But his mother had said he was the responsible one, so he'd done it. He'd known she'd counted on him as she never had been able to count on his father. The man had always been at work, shirking his family responsibilities, which had fallen to Sam.

When he had seen Derek flailing in the water, something inside Sam had panicked. He had raced across the sand to save his little brother. It had been his fault that Derek had been there in the first place. When Sam had told him to go and play, he hadn't been careful enough to watch him.

Falling fully into the memory, Sam let it wash over him, as the sand and the tide had then.

He remembered diving into the water, frantic to save Derek. By the time he'd swum to where he had last seen Derek, Sam had been shaking from exertion. His muscles had cramped and he had gone under. But then he had seen Derek floating just under the surface. Somehow he had managed to pull Derek up. Other people, who had heard him yell, had come to their rescue and pulled them both from the water.

Exhausted from the rescue, Sam had barely crawled out of the water as the others had carried Derek's limp body onto the sand. "I have to save him," Sam remembered crying. With the knowledge of basic rescue, he'd tried to revive his brother. But it had been too late. Derek had died because of Sam.

Startled by the power the memory still had over him, Sam wiped a hand across his face and put the swing into motion. There was nothing he could have done to save Derek. Now, as a physician, he knew that, but at the time he had been just a big brother desperate to save his little brother.

He'd failed.

CHAPTER EIGHT

JIMMY returned to his bunkmates the next morning as if he hadn't had a life-threatening experience the night before.

Vicki watched him from across the lodge, playing and romping with his friends. "He's good as new," she said as Sam joined her, his mood somber.

"Kids are resilient. They bounce back from lots of things it would take adults weeks to recover from." Though Sam spoke normally, she knew he was feeling down about something. It was in his tone, in the way he avoided her gaze. She'd only seen him this way a few times in the past.

"So what's bothering you this morning?" she asked, hoping he'd take the opportunity to talk to her.

"Nothing." He ate his oatmeal and stared into the bowl.

"Aren't you the one who just told me that there's always something behind the nothing?" Even if they weren't going to be married any longer, she hoped that they could end it on good terms. Being with him at camp had shown her that some part of her was able to move on, be civil. Though she'd never forget about their life together, at least she was putting it in its proper place. Perhaps coming to camp hadn't been such a bad idea after all.

"Not for me."

"Oh, so you're immune to the problems the rest of us have?"

"Don't play amateur psychiatrist with me, Vick. It won't work."

"I'm not playing," she said, and leaned forward. "There's obviously something bothering you. What is it?"

"This isn't about you and me, so just leave it alone, will you?" He rose and took his tray to the kitchen. When he turned round she was right behind him. "What do you want?"

"You haven't shaved, you look like you've slept in your clothes, you're grumpy. What's the matter with you? You can't take care of anyone like this. Go take a shower and get yourself together."

"You're a fine one to tell me what to do. Leave it alone, Vicki, before I say something I'll regret." He strode away, but she followed, and they almost raced down the front steps of the lodge and across to the infirmary. She struggled to keep pace with him, but she was going to.

"The kids always come first in your life, you've made that clear. But whatever is eating you could affect your judgment." Did she have to worry about that, too?

"My judgment is fine. You're the one who is aggravating me."

Placing a hand on Sam's arm, she stopped and made him look at her. "What is the matter?" He'd always been straight forward, she could be, too.

"Don't do this to me, Vicki."

"Do what? I don't understand what's wrong." Vicki felt very frustrated that he was being so stubborn.

"You don't need to," he said. "None of this is your problem any more, right?"

"Yesterday you made me see that I was holding in too much. I know that it's going to take me a long time to get over having three miscarriages. I'm accepting that. But you don't seem to be able to talk about anything."

"I don't need to talk." Sam took a step across the room and shoved both hands through his hair. "I don't want to talk. This isn't about me."

"Then what's it about?"

"My brother, dammit." Sam cursed and spun away. "This isn't about you, doesn't concern you."

"It doesn't have to be about me. Do you think I'm so self-absorbed that I don't care about you at all?" She hadn't meant to confess that.

"I don't want to talk about it."

"But it sounds like you need to. What about your brother?"

Sam continued to pace. Although he opened his mouth several times and looked at her, he didn't speak. So much pain had been bottled up in him, and until last night he hadn't realized it. "I let him die."

"Sam!" Vicki reached out to him. "That's not true…"

"Yes. It was *my* fault that he drowned. I should have been more responsible. I should have watched him. I should have saved him." Sam looked away from her, the muscles in his jaw clenching as he tried to control his pain. Now she knew.

Vicki took his hand and led him to the porch swing. This was what they'd done back in the early days when they hadn't had enough money to scrape together for a movie. They'd sat, swung, talked. "Tell me what happened."

Reluctantly, Sam sat next to her. They didn't talk at first. They didn't touch. But, still, Sam connected with her in a way that he'd never connected with another person. He was going to miss that. If confession was good for her soul, it couldn't hurt his either.

"I was sixteen and should have been watching my brother. He was only ten." Sam started the story that he should have told Vicki a long time ago. Protecting her had become a way of life that he hadn't realized. Falling into the trap of overprotecting her was just as bad as the trap of ignoring people, as his father had done. Being a doctor and saving everyone he could sometimes made up for the mistake of letting his brother die. Sometimes, but not always.

When he, finished the story, he looked at Vicki. Tears filled her eyes. Something. A look of forgiveness that he had so badly needed when he had been sixteen swam in her eyes.

"It wasn't your fault, Sam. It wasn't."

He snorted and looked away, not convinced. "I was supposed to watch him. I didn't." He shrugged. "It's in the past and long gone." Talking about it never helped him. He was a man of action, not words. He needed to do something. Maybe he could get a bucket of balls and go to the batting cage again. Hitting always made him feel better.

"It's not over. We carry those scars with us for ever. You've carried yours long enough." She touched his hand. "Why don't you let yours go?"

"It's not that simple." Nothing in life was ever that simple.

"Why, because you've made a life out of being the saver of everyone to make up for Derek?"

"You don't understand. You've never been responsible for someone else's death." Even as he said the words, he knew they weren't fair, weren't right. After holding the thoughts close for so many years, they were hard to relinquish.

"I have," she said softly. "You know I have."

"It's not the same, Vicki! You didn't deliberately set out to have a miscarriage." How could she think the two were the same? They were poles apart in thinking sometimes. Maybe it was for the best that they went separate ways.

"No, I didn't, you're right. And you didn't deliberately set out to let Derek die, did you?"

"No, but—"

"Just leave it at that. Just think about that." She placed her fingers over his mouth.

He wanted to pull her against him, lose himself in the pleasure of her body, as he had so many times in the past. But now he couldn't. That wasn't the right thing to do. He had to work through this or the rest of his life was going to be miserable. He didn't want that either.

With a nod he set the swing in motion and brought Vicki against his side. "Just sit with me for a while, will you?"

"Sure." Vicki leaned against him, and for once the silence between them was peaceful.

That evening, with a lull between the clinic and bedtime, Vicki pulled out a professional nursing journal. She'd brought a pile of them to read over the summer because her nursing license was due for renewal in a few months. Just about every state required nurses to obtain continuing education, whether it was in person, on the internet, or via journals. As she flipped through the pages, she discovered the topic of Candidiasis.

This diagnosis was something she'd never heard of in her years of nursing practice or learned of in school, and it roused her curiosity. After reading intently for a few minutes, a bubble of heat pulsed in her chest and tears formed in her eyes. Hurriedly she wiped them away, only to have new ones rush out and drip onto her magazine. With an impatient hand she brushed them away before they marred the information she was suddenly desperate to have. Maybe there was hope after all. That's all she wanted—one ounce of hope.

Sam found her there when he returned from Gilbert's office a few minutes later. "Vicki? What's wrong?"

"Nothing." She looked at him and smiled through her tears. "Nothing at all."

He frowned. Why was she crying and smiling at the same time? Could women be more confusing? No wonder men hadn't figured them out yet.

Vicki rose from the table, grabbed a paper towel and blew her nose. "I think I just figured out what's wrong with me."

She shook her head in denial as if she still couldn't believe it. Whatever *it* was.

"There's nothing wrong with you," Sam

said. He'd thought she'd started to heal, but maybe he was wrong, maybe she'd never get over losing the babies. "You've got to believe it."

"Yes, there is." Choked up by emotions bubbling in her, she couldn't speak and pushed the magazine toward him. Sam leaned over and looked at the magazine covered with wet spots. After reading for a few seconds he sat at the table, read some more, and then looked up at her, confusion written clearly on his face. "What *is* this?"

"It's the monthly topic in my nursing journal. Candidiasis is a systemic infection that causes all kinds of serious problems. Problems like miscarriages. I was catching up on my reading, and that's the one I opened." She gave a quick laugh and wiped fresh tears away. "Oh, my God. I think this has been my problem, Sam. All these years. The doctors, the tests, the frustration and disappointments may be from candidiasis." Unable to contain the sudden energy in her, she paced back and forth.

Sam watched her excitement with concern. "Don't get your hopes up just yet. If everyone who's seen you hasn't figured this out, how do you know it's true? How do you find out if you have it or not?"

"I don't know yet. I need to finish the article!" She sat and pulled the magazine toward her. "But I think it's promising." With a trembling hand she flipped the page to a lengthy outline of symptoms. "Listen to this. 'Irritable bowel syndrome, hormonal variances, chronic fatigue, thyroid, infertility issues, and miscarriages.' I've had all of these and so many others they list." Maybe, just maybe, this was the answer to her prayers. Tears again filled her eyes, but now they were tears of hope. "Even if I can never have a child, at least now I might know why I can't."

"Possibly. You need to get tested. If only for your peace of mind." Sam clutched her hand, and then dragged her into a quick hug. "Finish the article, and then I want to read it. There has to be more to it than that."

"Since you're here, why don't you sit down and I can read it aloud?" Right now she needed his support and friendship, just to get through these next few minutes.

Sam grabbed a soft drink from the refrigerator. "Go ahead. I used to love it when you read to me in the car."

Vicki poured a glass of water and then began to read. When she'd finished the article, they sat in silence, stunned at what the information could lead to.

"I don't understand why this isn't recognized more readily," Vicki said, frustrated and confused. "How many thousands of women go through this year after year without knowing what's wrong with them?" If only she'd known. If only she'd had an idea that something like this could have caused her physical problems, that it wasn't just her.

"The article said that symptoms can be so vague it takes someone who specializes in this to really figure it out. I know I've never heard of it, and I attend national education work-shops every year." Sam shook his head and frowned, thinking.

"I want to go to the hospital and get my blood checked right now." Vicki stood, needing something to do with the renewed energy rolling around in her.

"Considering that it's near midnight, I don't think it's a good idea. The required live blood cell test might not be available in such a small town."

"I know, I know. But I want to act right away." She paced back and forth in the small room.

"You will. If you'd like, I'll cover morning clinic and watch the infirmary until you get back."

"Oh, thank you, Sam. This means so much to me." On impulse, she leaned over and pressed her cheek to his. The touch of his skin against hers stirred feelings that made her want to reach out to him. But, she rationalized, it was probably just the excitement of the new discovery. Perhaps someday they could be friends again. The way they used to be, before all of the pain they had gone through.

As she leaned into him, Sam tucked his head in toward her neck and pressed his lips against her soft skin. A breath of a sigh parted her lips, and she closed her eyes, reveling in the sensations of his mouth against her. Sam scooped his hands beneath her hair and tilted her face to his. Gently, his lips touched hers in the softest kiss she'd ever known. Tears moistened her eyes again. She was just too emotional right now to think straight. Having Sam this close to her wasn't going to do either of them any good.

Somehow her mouth parted beneath his even as her hands reached to push him away. The memory of their shared passion blossomed in her chest, and she sank into Sam's arms, needing him desperately. A groan rumbled deep in Sam's throat as Vicki wrapped her arms around his shoulders. They were as solid as she remembered. Pressed against him, she explored the warmth of his mouth with her tongue. Jolts of desire shot through her as he answered her kiss.

Sam moved one hand to the small of her back and the other cupped her head as he deepened the kiss. Electricity sizzled between them in the small kitchen. Sex had never been their problem.

Shaking with needs she knew Sam could satisfy, Vicki pulled away from him, afraid to let him into her tightly controlled world. Afraid to get hurt again. Afraid to feel again. Afraid to hope again. If she didn't hope, she wouldn't suffer. Wide-eyed, she drew in a deep breath. "Wow."

"Vicki," he whispered, his eyes dark with desire, his breathing as erratic as hers. His heart raced beneath her palm. "Will you stay with me? Just tonight?"

"I can't." She shook her head. "This just felt…like we used to. For a moment I missed that." With her gaze downcast, she picked up the journal, needing to hold something in her hands or she was going to reach out for him. She couldn't do that ever again. Though need trembled inside her, she fought it, determined to break her dependence on Sam.

"Me, too. We were good together once,

weren't we?" he asked with a lopsided smile, his gaze soft as he ran a finger across her cheek.

"We were." If they hadn't been, leaving him wouldn't be so painful now.

With a nod he stood, and the tension between them evaporated. "Are you going to try to get some sleep?" He glanced as his watch, and his brows twitched upward. "It's later than I thought."

"No. I couldn't sleep now, I'm too wired. Can I borrow your laptop? I want to do some internet searching for candidiasis and see what else I can find out. There's got to be more information out there, maybe something on diagnosis and treatment." She felt as if she were at the crossroads of an answer. She just needed to take the right path to find it.

"Sure. Having more information would be good." Sam paused. He didn't want her to get her hopes up, but he knew he wouldn't be able to stop her. He just hoped it wasn't all in vain. "Good night, Vick."

"'Night," she said, and watched him walk down the hall, then veer off the other direction. "I thought you were going to bed," she said.

Sam turned back and snorted a laugh. "Cold shower first."

"Oh," Vicki said, and dropped her gaze. A small ball of pleasure that she couldn't suppress formed in her chest. She had no right to it, but the thought pleased her that she could affect Sam so quickly.

Needing the distraction more than ever, she retrieved Sam's laptop from its case and connected to the internet.

CHAPTER NINE

WHEN Sam got up the next morning he found Vicki sprawled across the kitchen table, asleep. Seeing her passed out on the table reminded Sam of their college days, studying for exams. Nursing school was nearly as tough as medical school, and Vicki had pulled many all-nighters for particularly difficult courses.

With a gentle hand on her shoulder, Sam nudged Vicki awake. She sat up and blinked to clear her vision, then focused on his face. "Oh, hi," she said in a husky morning voice. "Did I fall asleep?"

"Apparently. You have the imprint of your

watch on your cheek." Sam poured a glass of water and handed it to her, then readied the coffee-pot for the morning. "You can hit the shower first if you want, and I'll put some coffee on." He needed the distraction. Mornings had been one of their few times together, especially on lazy weekends.

"Thanks. I think I'll do that."

After breakfast Sam watched her go, feeling somewhat puzzled at his reaction to the possible candidiasis diagnosis. Perhaps this was the final piece of her puzzle. But he couldn't help worrying that she was giving herself false hope. He didn't want her to be disappointed. But, then, if she found the answers she was looking for, maybe things could be different between them. Whatever the outcome, although this wasn't his area of expertise, he would help her find some answers if she'd let him.

The screen door opened, distracting Sam from his thoughts. Emily and her two friends arrived. "So how are you, Emily?" The mishap hadn't done her any permanent damage. Just an overnight stay in the hospital.

"Good. But I'm never going near a horse again!" she exclaimed with a final gesture. "No way."

"That's not right," Sam said, and made a silly sad face that elicited the hoped-for giggle from her. "What if your horse misses you?"

"Misses me? A horse can't *miss* anyone," she said, and rolled her eyes at her friends, who laughed in response.

"That's not true. Horses have feelings, too. Have you checked to see if your horse had any injuries from the fall? Or wondered who has been caring for him since you've not been able to?" There was a serious side to this conversation as well.

Emily frowned, and her glance bounced away from Sam's. "Uh, no." She gave a quick shrug, as if it was unimportant. "Isn't there someone at the stables to do that stuff?"

"So, you were just thinking about how cool it is to have a hot-pink cast on your arm, weren't you?" What was it with girls and pink things? Sam didn't get it. His entire life wasn't planned around blue, so why did girls do the pink thing? Maybe if he'd had a baby girl he could understand it better.

Emily said "Duh" the way only teenagers could. "Well, pink is the cool color this year."

"Well, I didn't know that. So you'll be fashionable until your cast comes off, then what?" He checked her pulse and blood pressure while they chatted. Everything normal, just as he had expected. Now it was her mental health that he focused on. As he'd wished someone had focused on his long ago. If someone had followed up with him after Derek's drowning, maybe his life would have taken a different turn. Maybe he wouldn't be where he was now. Who knew?

"I don't know. Can I have another one put on?" Hope sparkled in her eyes. "One that I can, like, take off when it itches?"

"Nope. Sorry. One cast per customer. When it's off, you're done." Sam handed over her morning medications with a glass of water and thought about the past as he dealt with Emily's situation. "I think you need to go see your horse."

Tears flooded her eyes, and she shook her head. "No. I'm *afraid* of him. What if he falls on me again? I could...I could die!" Emily sobbed into her hands, drama in every gesture.

Sam had never been good with girl tears. Especially with hormonal preteens who tried to manipulate adults with them. Knowing he was being manipulated didn't stop him from buckling under the pressure. He needed to dig out his rusty psychiatric skills if he were really going to help her.

"OK. For the morning you're off the hook, but after lunch I want you down at the stables, making friends with that horse again." He pulled a prescription pad from the desk and scribbled on it.

Emily took it from him and read it. "A therapeutic ride? What's this?"

Tears swam again in her eyes, but he ignored them. "Get on that horse," Sam said, trying to be stern without being harsh.

"OK. I'll try." She wiped away her tears and hiccuped in a shaky breath. "But if I get killed, it's your fault."

Sam suddenly felt the urge to roll his eyes, too, but resisted being drawn into the melodrama. Though Emily nodded, Sam wasn't convinced she would go through with it. "What's his name anyway?"

"Whose name?" She blinked, her face blank.

"The horse's." Be calm, patient, Sam reminded himself.

"Oh. Buddy." She glanced away again, unable to hold Sam's gaze.

"To be sure you're not afraid of Buddy, I'll meet you there," he said, and escorted her to the infirmary door. "You've got ten minutes after lunch to change, then I want to see you on Buddy."

The smug look on Emily's face crashed to a shocked surprise. "You're gonna check up on me?"

"Sure. Just to make sure you're not afraid. See you then," Sam said, and the girls left the infirmary.

After lunch Sam was about to go to the stables to follow up with Emily when Vicki arrived.

"So how did it go?" he asked. By the glum look on Vicki's face and the flat light in her eyes, he guessed not well. Though he wished he could take some of her pain away, he knew she had to walk this path by herself. He could be there to pick up the pieces, but that was all.

"Terrible. I waited all morning for someone to figure out if they can do the test, and they can't. No one I talked to had a clue if there's anyone in the area who does the testing, and they've never even heard of candidiasis." She blew out a long breath trying to shake off the irritation.

"I'm sorry, Vick. I had hoped they could help you out." He could see the disappointment on her face, and he longed to do something about it. Maybe there was something.

"I'm so frustrated. Here I have all this information, and I can't do anything with it."

She was pacing back and forth in front of

Sam when an idea came to him. "I was going to meet Emily at the stables, but if you want to do that for me, I can make some calls. I've got a few friends in epidemiology who might be able to help." What could the offer hurt?

"Oh, Sam!" She clutched his arm against her, her eyes sparkling as he'd not seen in months. "If you could, I would be eternally grateful to you."

The pleasure on her face was more beautiful than he could have imagined. Keeping it there would be worth anything he had to do. "I'll try. "

"Why were you meeting Emily? Is she having problems with her arm?" She released him, but he still felt the pressure from her hand.

"Since the fall she's been resisting riding her horse. She says she's afraid of him. I told her I would come to the stables and help, so she wouldn't be afraid." Wanting to reach out to her again, he placed a hand on the back of her neck where the skin was warm and sensitive. "I really should have thought about this sooner. Post-traumatic stress syndrome can come in all shapes and sizes."

"You're right." Vicki nodded. The sparkle in her eyes changed, and sadness took its place as she stared at him. "I don't suppose after the accident with Derek anyone helped you, did they?"

She knew him. Hiding anything from her was futile, he'd been stupid to even try. "No. That's why I think that getting Emily back on Buddy is so important. Even if there weren't fatal consequences, the accident could have far-reaching results."

"Great idea. You should be a doctor." She gave him a playful elbow in the ribs, then scooted away. Vicki rubbed her hands together and the gleam returned to her eyes.

The pang in Sam's heart almost left him breathless as he stared at her. Unfulfilled longing for her rose within him. But he'd gone too far, said too many hurtful things for her to forgive him. He knew it. Maybe somehow he could make it up to her. If finding help for her possible condition was the only thing he could do, then he'd do it and walk away with peace in his heart.

"Just let me at her. I'll get her on that horse." She started toward the stables, but turned back. "Let me know the *second* you find anything out. Page me over the intercom if you have to. I want to know, no matter what it is."

"I will," he said with a quiet laugh at her enthusiasm, and watched her jog away. He hoped he could find something useful for her. The disappointment that had been in her eyes moments ago was something he wanted to erase for ever, but he didn't know whether he had the power to do that or not.

Later, after dozens of calls to colleagues and friends, Sam was no closer to finding a useful source of information than when he'd started. Most of his colleagues were as in the dark as he and Vicki about candidiasis. He even resorted to searching the local phone book. When that failed, he turned to the internet again. Searching, redefining the search, and searching again was about to make him throw the computer into the lake from sheer frustration. Too many ambiguous hits or nothing at all.

Then something appeared on the screen that looked more promising than the thousands of others.

One lone herbalist in Fryeburg, Maine, was listed with live blood cell testing as a specialty. Sam felt like he'd won the lottery. The woman listed might not be able to treat Vicki, but she sure could offer a diagnosis. At last, it was a first step.

Sam dialed the listed number. When the message-machine clicked on, he realized the entire afternoon had passed without Vicki's return. He looked at his watch. Almost five p.m. Giving in to a yawn, Sam stood and shook the life back into his cramped fingers.

Ambling down the hill toward the stables, Sam wanted to see how Vicki was handling the little drama queen and her horse. As he imagined all the creative excuses Emily could probably come up with not to make friends with Buddy, he chuckled. But then he stopped as a vision came into view.

Vicki was on a horse. Although she hadn't ridden regularly for a few years, she rode the palomino mare around the ring full of the life he had once fallen for. Emily looked on from her perch atop the fence.

At the end of the small performance of basic dressage techniques, Vicki and the horse took a bow. Emily clapped and Sam joined in, the lump in his throat prohibiting speech. Coming to camp, though unplanned, was obviously doing Vicki some good.

Pride in her swelled in his chest as she trotted around the ring. He stopped, admiring what a beautiful picture she made atop the horse. Charlie bounded away from him and shuffled to the edge of the arena. Vicki looked up and waved to Sam with a huge grin lighting up her face, then she dismounted.

"I knew if Charlie was here, you weren't far off." She hurried to the fence and crawled through. "Did you find anything? Tell me what you found." She tugged on his arm like an impatient child.

Sam laughed, enjoying the pleasure of it through his whole body. "I thought you were supposed to be helping Emily ride, not taking the horse for yourself," he said with a grin, trying to hide his reaction.

"Sam Walker! Stop teasing and tell me right now!"

He smiled, pleased with her reaction. "Found one. A herbalist in Fryeburg." Giving her the good news gave him such pleasure. For the first time in a long time he could say he felt good about something.

"Oh, great! But in Fryeburg? I'm surprised. That's such a small town."

"Big enough to support a herbalist. That's all we need."

"We're going to pack it in," the horse trainer said as Emily jumped from the railing. "It's almost time for dinner."

"OK, see you then," Vicki said with a wave, then turned back to Sam. "So when can I see him or her?"

"It's a her. Shelby McDonald. But I think she's gone for the day." The voice mail he'd left said it was urgent, so he hoped she would respond quickly.

"Darn. I was hoping that we could talk to her as soon as possible." Vicki puffed out her lower lip in a fake pout.

"Guess not today." Sam shook his head. "It won't be long now, and you'll know something."

Vicki crossed the first and second fingers of both hands and held them up for luck. "Here's to Shelby McDonald." She paused. "And to you for finding her."

The paging system blared out. "Chow time, boys and girls. Anyone wanting to eat should get to the lodge, pronto!" Bear's unmistakable voice made the loud and clear announcement. Lines of campers started forming outside the doors to the lodge.

"Have you eaten?" Sam asked, as he realized he hadn't had anything either.

"I ate some peanut-butter crackers, but that's it." She placed a hand over her abdomen. "I'm starved."

"Well, if you're up for it, I'll run to town, get a pizza, some wine, and we can eat in the infirmary." Where the suggestion had come from he didn't know, but the words were out before he could even think of retracting them.

"Sound's great. I'm going to wash up. By then I'll be way past ready for food."

Before Sam had time to react, she raced up the hill.

CHAPTER TEN

SAM opened the bottle of wine with fingers that fumbled on the opener. Why he had started to sweat over having a simple dinner with Vicki, he didn't know, couldn't imagine.

Something was happening that he wasn't prepared for and it scared him.

"Hey, the pizza smells great," Vicki said as she entered the small kitchen, smelling clean and fresh from the shower.

Sam handed her a glass of wine. "Remember the shop we used to go to every year? It's still there. I can't believe it. The owners are in their nineties, I think." He shook his head. "I had to yell three times to get him to understand that you actually *like* anchovies."

Vicki sipped her wine with a small chuckle, and he could see the laughter in her eyes.

"It's good to see you smile again, Vick. I know times have been hard on you, and I've been a bastard to live with." Sam sat, unprepared for the sudden confession that seemed to pour out of him. "I want you to know I'm sorry. For years I took it for granted that you would always be there, that you understood my work life, and that you didn't need much from me. You were independent and happy."

Unable to meet her eyes just yet, he picked up a slice of pizza and slid it in front of him. But she deserved an explanation, she deserved his honesty, not the lame excuses he'd given her over the years.

"I just want you to know that I'm very sorry to have taken you for granted and not been there for you. You deserve better than that."

Stunned, Vicki stared at him. Unable to hold off the flood of emotions, her eyes teared, and her chin trembled. "I never thought I'd hear you say that," she whispered, and set her wine down. "Never."

Sam took her hand and she held it tight. "It seems I'm having to learn a lot this summer. And being remote, being like my father...I don't want to be that way any more, Vick."

A gaggle of voices filled the infirmary as the children for the evening clinic filed in.

Vicki wiped her eyes with the heels of her hands. "Thank you. That means a lot to me." She stood. "I'll do the clinic and be back in a little bit. Can you keep the pizza warm for me?"

"Sure." Sam nodded and watched her go into the main room.

"So how's everyone tonight?" she asked in

a too-bright voice. He could tell she was trying hard to keep it together, not show her emotions in front of the children. She was definitely stronger than she knew.

With the business of camp activities and mending bumps and bruises, Vicki tried to forget about everything except what was in front of her. Some days she kept to herself, needing the time alone, and other days she joined in with the campers, losing herself in a project.

After a return call from the herbalist, Sam made an appointment to take Vicki to Fryeburg for testing. The next day was Saturday and the entire camp packed up to spend the day at another camp, engaged in intramural sports, picnics, and an evening dance. They were going to have a fun-filled day, giving Sam and Vicki a rare day off together.

"Got any plans today?" Sam asked her over breakfast. The surprise he kept was killing him. But he wanted to give it to Vicki and draw out the satisfaction as long as he could.

"Nothing special. Why?"

"Since the kids won't be back until late tonight we aren't needed in camp. Want to go shopping?"

"Sure, but… Wait a minute. You hate shopping. What's up?" Vicki narrowed her eyes at him, assessing, trying to figure him out. Keeping secrets from her was never going to be easy.

"There is a town in New Hampshire filled with outlets and New Hampshire is a tax-free state. Even *shoe* outlets." Sam could almost hear the wheels spinning in Vicki's mind, and he fought to control the grin that longed to burst onto his face.

"Where?"

Amusement glittered in her eyes. He could almost see her planning out her attack. "I'm not telling you."

"Then how am I supposed to indulge my shopping gene?" Hands on her hips, she stared at him.

"I'll take you. We'll spend the day, have lunch, explore, then come back tonight before the kids are back."

Vicki chewed on her lower lip. She always did that when she really wanted something, but didn't want to admit it. When she looked up at him he knew he had her, and the guilt that had lived inside him for so long began to ease. He wanted to do this for her. He needed to do it for her, but the side effects of it were long reaching, to ease his own pain.

"What about Charlie?" Vicki asked.

"He can stay with Bear for the day."

"OK. And we're standing here because…"

Sam grabbed her hand, she grabbed her purse, and they were out the door. An hour later they crossed the state line into Conway, New Hampshire, and the land of shopping outlets. By noon Sam's truck was full of shopping bags, parcels of early Christmas shopping and, of course, shoeboxes.

"By the way, did I tell you the second part of today's adventure? We have to make a stop in a little town on the way back. You might have heard of it. Fryeburg." He could no longer suppress his grin.

"Sam!" She slapped her hand on his thigh. "Are we seeing Shelby?"

"We are." He shot a sideways glance at her, then returned his attention to the road. "I hope that was OK. I know you don't like surprises, but this was just too good to pass up." He knew she hated him making decisions for her and he didn't want to go there again.

"Are you kidding?" She shifted in her seat, and fiddled with the handle of her purse. "I'm a little more open to surprises now than I used to be."

"Good."

Vicki fidgeted in the seat, unable to sit still and unable to contain the excitement bubbling in every vein of her body. Moments later Sam consulted his GPS unit and negotiated the remainder of the way to the herbalist's office in minutes. "I love this thing," he said, and patted the GPS unit. "You can find anywhere without a map."

"Men and their toys," Vicki said with a smile.

Though the words were playful, he sensed the tension in her voice and in the stiff lines of her body. He knew she was frightened. But he was going to be with her every step of the way, just like he'd promised, and this was one promise he wouldn't break. As he stopped the truck and turned off the engine, she grabbed her purse and dashed from the truck. The office turned out to be a private home with a fanciful, hand-painted sign that simply read, HERBALIST. At Vicki's knock, the door opened.

"Hello? You must be Vicki and Sam." The pretty brunette held the door open for them to enter. "I'm Shelby."

"Thank you," Vicki said. "I'm so thankful you had an opening today."

"My pleasure. Let's go into the office and get started. From what Sam said on the phone, I know you are eager for some results."

After they were seated in a small but comfortable office, Shelby started the session. "All I need from you now is one drop of blood." She reached for Vicki's hand and cleansed one finger with an alcohol swab. Shelby used a tiny lancet to prick Vicki's finger and squeezed a drop of blood onto a microscope slide, placed another on top and slid it into the high-power microscope viewer. "Here it is," Shelby said, as she adjusted the monitor. "It's connected to the screen so that you can see everything I see."

Vicki's future was in that single drop of blood.

Vicki and Sam drove in silence, mulling over all the overwhelming information Shelby had given them. They had spent two hours with her as Shelby explained every detail.

Vicki definitely had a significant case of candidiasis. After the grilling Sam had given Shelby, even he had been impressed with the scientific nature of Shelby's assessment. Vicki and Sam had both been through biochemistry and understood how the blood system worked, what bacteria, viruses, and yeasts looked like. They recognized everything Shelby had shown them and her explanation of how the biology worked also made sense.

Armed with a batch of herbal tea designed to kill the Candida yeast and flush it out of Vicki's system, the journey to a cure had begun.

"How are you doing?" Sam asked, and circled Fryeburg for the fifth time.

"I don't know. I don't know what to think, what to feel. But at least now I know what to do." She sighed as tears clouded her eyes, but she was determined not to give in to the depression that had taken over her life for the last few months. "I'm kinda disappointed this will never completely go away, though. I had hoped…" Numb from the onslaught of emotions tumbling around inside her, Vicki laid her head back against the headrest and closed her eyes.

"It's a start, Vicki. Now you know how to

treat the condition and can start feeling whole again. That's the important part."

"You're right." She nodded. "You're right. It's a new beginning for me."

Sam glanced at her, but kept an eye on the sky, which was changing from a beautiful blue to a boiling mass of gray. A storm crowding through the mountains darkened the late afternoon sky. "I know you're tired, but why don't we have something to eat before heading back to camp?" When in doubt, offer food.

"Sure." She shrugged as the heavy blanket of depression covered her again, the cloudy afternoon only adding to the effect.

Sam drove down the main street of Fryeburg and stopped at an inn.

The charming three-story Victorian glowed with light from within. Single candles in every window gave the house an old-world charm and a little of her dark mood lifted. An hour or so in a beautiful setting would definitely improve her disposition. "Oh, this is lovely, Sam. Thank you."

As soon as they were seated, thunder roared overhead and the skies broke open. Rain pelted the roof and frothed in torrents down the windows, but the sturdy building kept the occupants inside warm and dry. A fire burned in the hearth, adding a romantic intimacy, and they seemed encased in a cocoon protected from the elements. Time stilled.

While sitting at the table closest to the fire, having a quiet meal, something unraveled in Vicki. The tightness that had remained between her shoulder blades for months now eased. The tension in her neck also relaxed, and her breathing felt smoother. Though they were physical issues, she sensed that the root cause was emotional. Part of her change she knew was Sam. Part of it was her. They'd both changed. She knew she wasn't as bitter, and Sam? Well, Sam had softened. The rough edges of him that always hurt her had gone.

This time, when she'd needed him, he had been there. Without hesitation he was there to help her. At the start of the time at camp she'd have said she couldn't have lived with him. Now? Now she didn't know if she could live without him in her life.

While enjoying a dessert of cheesecake topped with locally grown strawberries bursting with flavor, Vicki looked at Sam as if seeing him for the first time. How on earth was she going to pretend for the rest of her life that she didn't want him? That he was no longer what she needed?

As Sam took her hand in his and offered her the last spoonful from his plate, the owner of the inn burst into the dining room with a portable phone pressed to her ear. "Oh, dear.

Oh, dear." She pulled back a lace curtain to look outside.

"I wonder what's going on," Vicki said as she watched the woman fret, thankful for the distraction. Her thoughts were definitely going the wrong direction.

The woman clicked off the phone and turned to the diners with a tight smile. "Well, I'm not sure how to tell you this, but you are all going to have to stay the night here," she said.

Vicki sat upright. "Why? What's going on?"

"The bridge over the river has been washed out. If you were headed anywhere down east, you're stuck here."

"Washed out? How are we going to get back to camp?" Vicki glanced at Sam, thinking of his GPS navigation system. Would it work in a storm like this? Could they go around this area?

"From what she says, we aren't," Sam said,

and leaned back in his chair, looking undisturbed by the news.

"But the kids…" Who would run the clinic if they weren't there? Medical personnel had to be present for administration of medications. If she and Sam were here, there was no one else.

"Are probably not going anywhere either. Don't worry. Let me call Gil and see if they are stranded, too."

After a short, broken conversation with Gil, Sam clicked off his cellphone. "They're stuck, too. They had a flash flood above the camp where they are."

Vicki slapped a hand over her heart and sighed in relief. "I'm so glad we sent the meds with the kids. The nurses at the other camp can help get them sorted out."

"See? You were right." Sam nodded and addressed the inn owner. "So, Mrs Butler, what do you have in the way of rooms tonight?"

"Oh, I have a lovely suite for you two."

"Sam, I don't have a nightgown, or a tooth-brush, or anything." Women needed stuff to survive, even for a short trip. Was that anxiety throbbing through her veins or anticipation? She didn't want to know, she didn't want to guess, she didn't... Yes, she wanted him.

"Didn't I see you just buy a pair of silk pajamas today?"

"Yes, but they're a Christmas present for Dotty. I can't wear them." An excuse or a reason? Oh, she wanted him.

"Wear them. You can go shopping again tomorrow and buy another pair."

When Sam and Vicki entered their suite on the third floor, Vicki stopped in the doorway, and stared. She knew that somehow she had been transported back in time to the very suite that she and Sam had shared on their wedding night. Although it wasn't, in fact, the same place, every polished wooden surface of antique furniture gleamed and a light fragrance of lemon hung in the air, transporting Vicki's senses. White, hand-crocheted doilies supported lamps, vases, and other decorative items from a bygone era, epitomizing that old world charm Vicki had noticed downstairs.

Vicki walked to the bureau and lifted the crystal lid off a delicate jewel box that played a song equally as delicate. "Oh, Sam. This is just…beautiful," she whispered, knowing her excuses were gone. Anticipation hummed along her skin, and Sam hadn't touched her yet. Without looking at him, she sensed his needs were as great as hers.

Sam stepped up behind her and rested his hands on her shoulders, the warmth from him seeping into her skin. She closed her eyes, savoring the warmth, the heat, and the strength of him so close. The barriers she'd erected against him, against herself, began to crumble.

"Remind you of anything?" he asked, his voice husky in her ear, the heat of his breath sending tingles of desire across her skin.

"Our honeymoon." Desire took her places she'd thought she had forgotten about. Her body ached for Sam to touch her.

"I have an image in my mind of you in your gown, standing so lovely beside the bed as I undressed every layer of satin and lace." The tremor in his hands moved through her. He was as nervous and eager as she was.

"I remember," she said, and licked her dry lips, trying to push away the desire pulsing beneath the surface, but she couldn't. The electricity in the air wasn't just from the storm outside. It crackled between them. She wanted more.

"I think you did it in purpose," he said with a slight chuckle as he nuzzled her ear. "Took for ever to get through all those layers to find you."

Remembering, she laughed and tears filled her eyes at the same time. "I did. I wanted you to work for it."

"I want to do it all over again. Now." Sam's voice took on a rough edge, the emotion in him spilling over.

"Sam…" Wide-eyed, she stared at him in the mirror. "I…"

"Give me tonight, Vicki. I need us together, one last time." The ache in Sam's voice filled her mind, pushing away lingering doubts and the tension of the last few months. He needed her. Finally, he needed her, and it wasn't just about sex.

The longing for Sam, her friend, her lover, her husband, overpowered everything, and she turned in his arms to face him. "I don't want to need you, and I don't want to feel this way about you. But I do need you." Her breath caught in her throat, and her voice dropped to a mere whisper. "I do." It was the final admission, and the last barrier against him shattered.

"No promises," he said. "Just tonight."

CHAPTER ELEVEN

"JUST tonight." It was all she could give him right now.

Sam looked deeply into her eyes, his own desire and need reflected there. His hands cupped her face while he opened his mouth and took hers. Clasping his wrists, she answered him.

Sam groaned deep in his throat and broke the kiss. Gasping for air, he pulled her hard against him. The tremors of his body let her know he was just as affected as she was. Exploring his lips with her tongue, she couldn't wait any longer. "Kiss me, Sam."

Teasing, tasting, testing, Sam's mouth created swirls of desire that flashed into a craving only he could satisfy.

The heat of his body fused with hers. She knew his need to feel their skin touch was as great as her own. Pulling back from him, she tore her shirt off and urgently reached for Sam's.

Unwilling to relinquish her for even a moment, he kissed her neck, pressed his face against her warm skin, and savored the sweet scent of her.

"You are so beautiful, Vicki." With a twist of his fingers the bra clasp sprang free, and he drew it down her arms, his nails lightly grazing her skin.

She shivered, but kept her gaze on him, the need in her eyes propelling him forward. Now he wasn't sure he needed to take it slowly. His mouth on hers again, he moved with her toward the bed and pulled her shorts and panties off while her hands worked the fastening of his shorts.

"Sam, I can't get it," Vicki said, her hands tugging frantically at his zipper.

With a groan of frustration he practically tore his shorts off and freed his skin to hers. Then her hands were on him and they tumbled across the bed.

Sam's weight felt so good. He pressed her deep into the down comforter. His urgent hands were touching, teasing, tantalizing her. With his knees between hers, he pressed her legs apart. Breaking free of the kiss, Sam trailed his tongue down her skin, leaving a moist mark that made her skin react with goose-bumps. The trail ended, and he scooped her nipple into his mouth, twirling his tongue around until the hard peak throbbed. This was what she needed, what she craved.

The taste and the feel of Vicki's skin against

his made Sam want to slow down, but her hands on him rendered him incapable of taking his time.

He suckled her nipples and stroked his mouth over her abdomen, relearning her shape and her textures. Without another thought he moved lower and tasted her again.

Vicki closed her eyes and fisted her hands into Sam's hair. With a few soft strokes of his tongue against her, she arched her back and shattered, the climax so intense a scream was almost torn from her. As the peak ended, Sam moved up again, and she clasped her legs around his hips pulling his body into hers. Sam filled her, just as she remembered. Just as she needed. As his breathing changed, so did hers, and he took her home again. Sam's hoarse cry in her ear and the stiffness of his movements only added to her satisfaction as she clung to him.

Vicki clasped her arms around Sam's neck and lost herself in his embrace. So many nights her dreams had taken her here, denying her the satisfaction of spending reality in Sam's arms. But now nothing else mattered, and she was his, as he was hers.

Outside, the night poured its worst down on them, and they drew on the energy from the storm to fuel their own storm of emotions.

Rolling with her, Sam brought her against his side.

Vicki couldn't speak. So much was happening inside her that she couldn't form a coherent thought.

"Are you OK?" he asked, and stroked her back with his fingers. He always did that after making love. She'd missed it.

Until now she hadn't realized how much. She nodded. "You?"

"Oh, yeah. I'm good."

And then the tears came. Unable to hold them back, Vicki gave in to the months of emotions she'd tried to deny. Sam tunneled one hand beneath her hair, and with his other arm he held her tight.

He didn't ask questions, he didn't talk, he didn't try to fix anything, he just held her and didn't let go.

Sam understood her tears better than she knew. The longing they each had for the good times was almost tangible. The sweetness of her, the strength of him, had somehow gotten lost in careers and angry words, losses and disappointments, until there had been nothing left.

Now? He didn't know, but he wanted…oh, he wanted again as he hadn't wanted ever in his life.

For a time they slept, curled together as they had in their early days. But the night was not over yet, and Sam stroked his fingers up her thigh, across her ribs and cupped her breast.

On a deep inhalation she opened her eyes and focused on his face as his thumb teased her nipple. He leaned into her, kissed her, stealing her breath.

Skin to skin they lay, Sam's hands and mouth ranging over every inch of her, relearning and remembering each taste, each curve, each pleasure point.

As he was about to join with her, a second of unwanted sanity stopped him. "What about…?"

"Birth control?" Vicki finished for him, her eyes now wide.

"Yes. Now's a really bad time to bring it up, but…"

"Check the bathroom cabinet. I saw some condoms in there when I was looking for a toothbrush." The idea hadn't occurred to her earlier. How could she have not remembered?

Sam planted a hard kiss to her mouth. "Don't

move a muscle," he instructed, and dashed to the bathroom.

Vicki bit back a laugh as she listened to Sam open the cabinet and rummage around, cursing the whole time. Then he was back in her arms, and she thought of nothing else except him. The tension of the last year faded from her mind and her body relaxed as Sam touched her.

Vicki pulled him over her and drew him into her body, gasping as he entered her, savoring the feel, the heat, the stretch of her body to accommodate him again. Heaven was here in this man's arms, and she savored every breath of it. As he moved, she clung to him, needing to lose herself in his embrace, wanting to give something back to him, even if it was for just one night. Wrapping herself around him, she tightened her grip on his hips, urging him to take her places she knew he could. As waves of pulsation crested over her, she cried out. Sam hurried the pace and took his own pleasure.

Twice more during the night they made love, each time with more desperation. As if each of them knew this was a time out of time, time that they could steal away from reality and indulge themselves without thoughts of the future.

Cocooned in the cozy little room at the top of the inn, time ceased to matter.

The next morning they showered together, subdued and lost in their own thoughts. Sam pulled Vicki against him, trembling as he held her while the water pelted them and steam rose in a soft mist.

Tears pricked Vicki's eyes. "This is it, isn't it?" she asked, her insides trembling, her legs weak.

"I won't say it's over. I can't." With all the ferocity of a man driven beyond his endurance, Sam took her against the wall of the shower, pouring everything he had into her. Vicki clung to him, letting him set the pace, their loving fierce. After the physical on-slaught had drained her of every ounce of energy, she hung limply in his embrace.

Not knowing what to feel, she pulled away from Sam and left the shower to dress.

Sam closed his eyes and allowed the water to wash over him. There was nothing left to say.

They pulled into camp just as the buses did. Kids poured out, finding friends and returning to their normally scheduled activities.

Vicki spent the remainder of the day recovering the medications from the children, reorganizing schedules, and trying to keep her mind busy enough to forget the overwhelming passion she and Sam had shared.

Unable to face a meal in the lodge with

everyone else, Vicki fixed herself a sandwich in the infirmary kitchen and rested a few minutes before the next clinic started. She also boiled water and brewed a cup of the herbal tea to treat the candidiasis.

Vicki was sitting on the porch swing, sipping her tea, when Sam emerged from the shower, his damp hair combed straight back from his face. She tried not to notice the clean fragrance that wafted off of him, like some exotic spice and soap mingled together, teasing her senses.

Sam's presence filled her with dread. When he looked down at her, she nearly bolted.

"We haven't had much time to talk," he began, twirling a lock of her hair between her fingers.

"I know. And I think we should." She reached up and removed her hair from his grasp.

"Last night—" he began.

"Was a mistake," she finished. She had to

finish it before Sam pulled her into his web any more.

"Vick—" Surprise and hurt mingled in his eyes.

"Let me finish. Please," she said, and drew a deep breath. "Making love with you last night was beautiful, but it shouldn't have happened. It was just circumstances that led us there. If we had been here in camp it wouldn't have happened." She had to believe it or she couldn't go on.

"You don't know that," he said, the set of his jaw hard. "We could have—"

"No, we wouldn't. We've grown apart, we're heading in different directions, we want different things now than we did when we were married." Vicki raked a frustrated hand through her hair. Why had she ever given in to Sam? Why couldn't she have been stronger in resisting her need for his touch?

"We're *still* married."

"Not for much longer," she said, and the knife of guilt slicing through her heart almost stopped her. "We can't go on like we're getting back together, because we aren't. You're more married to your job than you are to me. You always have been. That's not going to change when camp's over, and I can't compete with the children that so desperately need you."

"I know I have been, and I'm sorry. I can make it up to you."

"No, you can't. You can't change the past."

"If I could, I would, Vicki, I would. But I can learn from it. Make changes, make things different." The desperation in his voice made her ache.

"If we stayed together, I'd just hold you back. You know what you need, and it isn't me. Let me go, Sam. I don't love you any more." She rose, turning her head away, her breath panting from between her parted lips as she spoke the ultimate lie that would separate them for ever.

The sight of Sam's face, frozen in shock, would be always etched in her brain. "I don't believe you," he said. "That's not what last night told me."

"Denial won't get you very far in life," she said. "Go back to your work, the way you had planned." She hurried into the infirmary, sobs tearing at her throat, and she launched herself onto her bed.

Charlie nosed his way into the room and crawled up onto the bed with her. His furry warmth seeped into her flesh, and she clung to him and cried, letting go of Sam for the last time.

CHAPTER TWELVE

UNABLE to move, Sam remained on the swing. She'd done it again. Or maybe he'd done it to himself. Last night he'd reached out to her, opened himself to her emotionally, as he hadn't in years. And he'd thought… Dammit, he'd felt her response to him. He knew that she'd needed him as much as he'd needed her. So, now what? Just let her walk out of his life as if she meant nothing to him?

By God, that wasn't going to happen. He rose from the swing and it rocked madly back and forth out of sync. In a few steps he reached her door and opened it. There were not going to be any more barriers between them. Not if he could help it.

"What the hell is your problem?" he demanded. He wasn't going to be satisfied with the lame excuse she'd given him. It was a lie. It had to be.

Vicki rose from the bed, her hair scattered, her face red and wet with her tears. "Get out of my room."

"I'm not leaving without an explanation."

"Then I'll leave." Vicki tried to shoulder her way past him, but she didn't even make it to the door before Sam stepped inside and closed it.

"You're not going anywhere either. Not until we've worked this out. Somehow we have to work this out." He grabbed her shoulders and kept her in front of him.

"Let go of me." She struggled in his grip, but she couldn't release his hands.

"Stop it. Just stop it right now and look at me."

"No. Just leave it alone, Sam. We're not good together any more."

"No good together?" Sam gave a caustic laugh. "I thought we were always damned good together. Last night was especially remarkable."

"You know what I'm talking about," she said, and he finally released her, but remained in front of the door.

"Explain it to me again, because the first time wasn't clear enough." The muscles in his back twitched and his hands bunched into fists he shoved into his pockets. Maybe he just had to torture himself before he accepted the inevitable.

Three times she looked at him and opened her mouth, but nothing came out. And he waited. Tears filled her eyes and spilled over again, but still he waited.

"What if I'm pregnant?" she cried, her

hands over her cheeks. "Oh, my God, what if I'm pregnant?"

"We used protection…mostly," he finished, thinking of the first time they had made love.

"No, we didn't. Oh, Sam. We're on the verge of divorcing. What if…" Her breath hitched. "I won't be able to handle another disappointment, losing another baby. It's too painful."

Not knowing what to say, Sam stepped closer to her and brushed away her tears with his thumbs and tilted her face up to his. "If you are, we'll handle it *together.* We made it together. We'll deal with it together. I'm not going anywhere, I'll be here for you." The pain of losing Vicki and potentially losing another child, pounded at him. She was so fragile sometimes he felt he'd break her if he touched her. As gently as he could, he pressed a kiss to her lips, and she let him. "Everything will be fine." He hoped the words were really true.

"I'm just not strong enough to handle it any more. There have been too many disappointments, too many losses."

"What are you saying?" He held her away from him so he could look into her eyes.

"I'm saying that some days I just don't think I can face life any more and want to find a dark hole to hide in." With a small laugh and a watery smile she pulled away from him. "But what else am I going to do? Stay in bed all day and be depressed? That's not me either. There are kids out there that need my help, so I get out of bed and start again."

He wanted to tell her how proud of her he was, but he held back. He couldn't take that last step and bare his soul completely to her. Not when he wasn't sure how she would respond.

A knock on the door interrupted them. "Anybody here? Nurse Vicki? Doctor Sam?"

Vicki looked at Sam. "I forgot about the evening clinic." She rubbed her hands over her face. "Just a minute!"

"You look fine. I'll give you a hand."

"I'd like that." She put on a bright smile and opened the door. "OK, who's up first?"

Sam watched her transform from the tearful, anxious woman he'd held in his arms into a professional woman who knew exactly what she had to do. He just wished she could face their problems together with him with the same attitude. Maybe, given some time, she would.

"Who needs what? Dr Sam and Nurse Vicki are on the job," he said, taking his cue from Vicki. In seconds they were embroiled in the excited voices and unpredictable antics of the children.

They tried to forget about their night at the inn. Camp life kept them busy and everyone helped the continued clean-up from the fire. After a few days the underlying tension was almost unbearable and Vicki needed a break. "Sam, can you to take the after dinner clinic tonight?" Vicki asked.

She wore a plain white skirt and a blue T-shirt. Casual as always, but tonight something else was up. He could feel it.

"Sure." He watched as she gathered several items from the kitchen. A bottle of wine, two glasses and assorted chocolates made their way into a basket that Vicki hooked on her arm. Then she clicked her away across the tile floor in a pair of flimsy sandals. And perfume. Sam frowned. He couldn't recall her wearing perfume the entire time at camp. "Got a hot date?" Though he could have kicked himself for wanting to know…he wanted to know.

Vicki looked at him, her blue eyes amused. "Yes, with Ginny."

Sam watched her go, relief spinning in his gut. But it took the first kid blasting through the door of the infirmary after dinner for Sam to try and forget the sight of Vicki walking away.

Moments later Vicki knocked on Ginny's door.

"Come in," Ginny called from somewhere inside the rustic cabin at the edge of the lake. Vicki hadn't spend nearly enough time with her friend this summer and hoped tonight would make up for some of that. She entered through the squeaky screen door and let it fall shut behind her.

"It's me," Vicki said, and set the basket on a chair.

"Hi. I'm so glad you suggested this," Ginny said. "I need to take a break and talk to big people for a change." She laughed and hung a wet towel on a peg to dry.

After seating herself in one of the wooden

chairs, Vicki sighed. "I really need some girl time, too." Did she ever. After the last two weeks, she needed to talk to someone.

"OK, so what's going on?" Ginny asked, and pulled the two glasses from the basket while Vicki opened the bottle. "What kind of wine did you bring?"

"Riesling. Goes well with chocolate and deep sorrow."

"Uh-oh. What's going on?" Ginny opened the packet of chocolate and broke it into equal shares, then handed a portion to Vicki. "Not that I mind sharing wine and good chocolate with a friend, but this sounds serious."

Vicki contemplated her empty glass and then poured a measure for each of them. She frowned, pondering how to start the story as the chocolate melted in her fingers.

"Quit fidgeting and tell me what's happened." Ginny laughed.

"Sam and I made love." There. She'd said it. That meant it was real. "When the kids were stranded at the other camp, Sam and I went to Fryeberg."

"So what's wrong with that?" Ginny said, confusion in her voice. "You're married."

"But we're divorcing!" Why did everyone forget that part of the scenario? Vicki sipped her wine, then licked a drip of melted chocolate from her fingers.

"Why?" Ginny leaned forward, intent on hearing every word.

"Because I can't have children, because he's married to his job, not me, and because I want more out of life than a phone call that he's going to be working until midnight again!" The burst of emotion caught Vicki off guard and tears pricked her eyes.

"I'm sorry, Vicki." Ginny's intent gaze wouldn't let her go. "The children thing you can't fix, but what about adoption? What about one of these kids right here in camp that needs a good home and two loving parents?"

Vicki stared at Ginny. "I've never… We've never considered it." She sighed and wiped her eyes. "It's so much more than just the children issue. He's just not been there for me when I needed him. So many times his work has come first and I've been left to pick myself up alone." She shrugged. "I don't want to do it any more."

"I've almost died trying to have a child, and I can't do it again. I don't know what I'd do if I became pregnant again." What a nightmare that would be.

"Did you use protection?"

Though an indelicate discussion, Vicki wasn't uncomfortable talking about it with Ginny. "Most of the time."

Ginny laughed and slapped a hand on her

thigh. "You sound like a couple of teenagers who couldn't keep their hands off each other."

Vicki had to smile. "Well, that's basically what happened. We haven't been that…demonstrative for a long time. It was nice to just throw everything out the window."

"Including the condoms!"

"Ginny!" Vicki scolded, but couldn't find any heat in her words. How could she? She and Sam had taken a huge chance at having created another pregnancy, unwanted by either of them this time.

"What has he said?" Ginny's voice turned serious.

"He says he can live without children, but I see it in his eyes every time he looks at the kids we treat in the infirmary."

"What kind of look? Thankful they aren't his?" Ginny snorted.

"Ginny!" Vicki laughed and some of the

tension in her shoulders eased. Having a friend to sound things off to was good for her.

"Some of these kids are terrible. You should be glad they aren't yours."

"They can't help it. At least, some of them can't. Take Jimmy, for example, his is such a sad case—taken away from his father by the state." Vicki shook her head. "From what Jimmy said, however, it sounds like the best thing, but it's still so sad not to have any family."

"Yes, I heard." Ginny shook her head at the injustice of it all. "But this is what I'm saying, Vicki. He's an example of a child in need that you yourself could help if you did choose another route rather than pregnancy. But for now I bet you know someone who would be able to give little Jimmy a home."

"It's not like taking in a stray dog, Ginny."

"I know that," she said. "But a kid needs a

home. And I'm sure you know someone who has one. Between you and Sam you have the most extensive network of friends and colleagues I've ever seen." Ginny shook her head in disbelief.

"That will be one good thing about divorcing Sam," Vicki said, and her chin quivered.

"What?"

"My Christmas-card list will be down to nothing." Vicki said. And she started to cry.

"Come here." Ginny stood and opened her arms.

Vicki clutched her friend and sobbed. "It's wrong. Everything is wrong, and I don't know what to do." She pulled away and wiped her face.

"Do you still love him?" Ginny asked. "Can you live without him?"

"I…I…" Vicki hung her head and dropped back into the chair, her chin trembling.

"Sometimes I don't know any more," she whispered, unable to admit it out loud. "I'm so confused. Being with him was incredible, but how do I know if I'm thinking with my head and not my heart? What has thinking with my heart gotten me? Nothing but a whole lot of pain."

"I'm no psychologist, but it sounds to me like you need to find out what you really want. If you really want to leave Sam, do it, but do it for the right reasons." Ginny sipped her wine again and gave Vicki time to think.

The thought of leaving Sam for good, giving him up to another woman, letting go of their past together, was almost more than she could bear. "I've loved him for a very long time."

"Everyone goes through bad times in a marriage. You need to talk to Sam and figure out if you can make it work again."

Vicki leaned her head against the back of the chair and closed her eyes. "The other news is that

I may have discovered the reason for my miscarriages." At least there was good news to share.

"What?" Ginny shrieked. "That's fabulous. Tell me… What…? How…? Tell me, tell me, tell me."

Vicki related the story of her candidiasis discovery and Ginny flopped back into her chair, a stunned look on her face.

She twisted her glass, her hands trembling on the delicate stem, suddenly uninterested in the wine. "If I hadn't picked up that journal, I might never have known it could be responsible for miscarriages. That scares me more than anything."

"I'm astonished that no one ever caught this before. How did Sam react?"

Vicki grinned. "He grilled Shelby for two hours, but he was impressed with her findings."

"That man loves you," Ginny said, her voice gentle.

Tears flooded Vicki's eyes. "He's been married to his work, not me, for a long time. I don't think he knows what he wants any more than I do right now."

"You're not being fair to Sam and you're not giving him the chance he deserves," Ginny said, her voice quiet. "I've made my own marital mistakes, but you and Sam have been so good for so many years… Don't give up on him now. Don't give up on yourself either. Take a breath and give yourselves a chance. If you don't take the chance, you'll never know."

"I don't know if I have the strength to make it work." And she didn't.

Silence hovered over the small cabin for a few minutes. Changing the subject away from her personal life, Vicki asked, "So how is your crew doing this year? Any swim champs in the making?"

Ginny shook her head in disgust. "I'm surprised the lot of them haven't drowned yet. But there are a few who are ahead of the rest."

They talked for a while of camp life and other neutral topics. After two hours Vicki packed up the basket and returned to the infirmary. As she walked up the hill from the lake, twilight overtook the camp Vicki reveled in the familiarity of the place. She'd been working here for years and she knew every sound, from the squeaks of the lodge steps to the slam of the infirmary door, to the lap of rippling waves on the lake. In some ways this was her home more than her real home was. Each year loons nested on the peaceful lake, and Vicki cherished listening to their haunting morning calls. Spying a mated pair with their new brood was a special treat.

But as she approached the infirmary she found Sam rocking back and forth on the porch swing, and she stopped. She'd loved this man. He'd become a part of her, shaped her life, helped make her what she was. And now she was giving him up. Was that really the answer? Or did Ginny have some valid points? She bit her lip. Could she do it?

Vicki opened the infirmary door sat beside him on the swing.

"I've been doing some thinking," he said.

"So have I." Had she ever. Inside she trembled and her palms started to sweat. If she took this step, would she ever be able to go back? "Sam, I—"

Sam's cellphone went off. "Damn. Hang on a second." He answered it, spoke for a few seconds and then hung up. "Grab the E-kit. Bring it to Gil's. I think he's having a heart attack." Sam dashed toward the administrator's cabin, and Vicki rushed inside for the kit.

CHAPTER THIRTEEN

SHE burst through Gil's cottage to find Sam hovering over Gil's body on the floor. "Gil!"

"It's OK," Sam said and sat back. "I think he's just lost consciousness."

"But if he's fainted, that's bad," she said. "Have you called 911 yet?" There had to be a reason for such a condition change. She hoped Sam wasn't overlooking something because of his friendship with Gil.

"No." Sam ran a hand through his hair.

"Sam! What's the matter with you?" Had the man gone off the deep end? But as she watched him, she stopped. She'd always trusted his instincts in medical emergencies so why should she question them now? Calming herself down, she moved beside them and put the E-kit on the floor, opened it and hooked the oxygen mask to the tank out of habit. If Gil didn't need it, she could use some. The sudden exertion had made her dizzy and her heart was tripping over itself. "OK, what do you think's going on?" She took in a few cleansing breaths and tried to get her heart rate under control.

"I think he's had an anxiety attack." He motioned for the mask. "Good idea. Let's get some oxygen on him anyway."

"I'll get his vitals." After checking Gil's BP and pulse, Vicki relaxed again, though she was still puzzled. "You may be right. His pulse is a little elevated and his pressure's a little low, but nothing dangerous. An anxiety attack could definitely account for those changes." As always, the thought that Sam was right comforted her. Counting on him was something she had taken for granted over the years, but now found the stability of it almost refreshing.

A fluttering of Gil's eyelids indicated that he was starting to respond. Tentatively, he placed his hand over his forehead and offered a groan. "What happened?" He looked up at them, his eyes focusing.

"You fainted," Vicki said.

"I did not," Gil denied, and pushed the mask away from his face.

Sam chuckled and elbowed Vicki in the ribs. "Men don't *faint*. We *pass out*. It's more manly."

Incredulous, Vicki frowned and shook her head, indicating her serious lack of support of the male ego. "That's ridiculous. Gil, you fainted dead away on the floor." Men! Always conscious of their egos.

"You've obviously never lost your cookies

in a locker room full of jocks before," Gil said, and Sam nodded.

"I've never lost my cookies anywhere, thank you very much," she said with her nose in the air. *As if.*

Sam eased back onto his heels, looking at Vicki in disbelief. "Really? I remember holding a bucket for you the weekend you graduated from nursing school."

Vicki's face warmed, and she stood up, preferring not to remember it quite that way. "Don't you think we should help Gil, instead of reminiscing over various interpretations of the past?"

Sam chuckled and ruffled her hair. "For now." He helped Gil to a sitting position. Once reassured that the administrator had suffered no injuries from the fall, they moved him to the sofa.

"I don't need to lie down," Gil insisted. "I'm not an invalid, you know."

Sam sat on the coffee-table across from Gil. "So what were you doing that caused your trouble?"

"I was on the phone to that ridiculous insurance adjuster," Gil began. "He's actually thinking of recommending that we be dropped. 'Too much liability,' he said. Bah!" Gil shook his fist and his face reddened. "I'll give him some liability right up his nose!"

Sam cleared his throat, trying to hide his amusement. "And do you think this may have been the cause of your distress?"

"Just as I was about to tell him what he could do with his recommendation, my chest felt tight, and I couldn't breathe." Gil looked at the floor and his face returned to its natural color. "That's when I hung up on him and called you."

"I see," Sam said, and checked Gil's pulse again. "You'll be fine, provided you control your temper on the phone."

"I suppose I should call him back." Gil looked at the black phone on the end table.

"Only if you intend to keep your insurance with this company. It won't hurt you to play nice for a little while. Invite him up for a few days to see what we actually do here. It's harder to deny someone to their face." Sam had been around enough insurance companies to know how the game was played.

"Excellent suggestion," Gil said with a smile, and clapped a hand on Sam's shoulder. "You're full of good ideas."

Vicki stood and hefted the E-kit. "Why don't we get out of your hair?"

Gil reached for his phone. "Thank you for coming to see me. Come again some time," Gil said, as if they'd just had a lovely, planned visit.

"Uh, we will," Vicki said, and handed the kit to Sam as they walked out the door. She scratched her head. "That was strange. I hope he's really OK." The longer she knew men, the less she understood them.

"I'll check him again tomorrow, but I think it was just a panic attack."

"Your instincts have always been right, so I'll defer to you on this one," Vicki said. Being with Sam again, chasing down emergencies, made something in her heart flip. When dating, they had run ambulance rescues together, thriving on the adrenaline rush it had given them. Nostalgia seeped into Vicki's mind as she thought back to that time. Sam had been so hot to go after critical emergency calls, wanting to be first at the scene, first to bring in the emergencies, and the first to call the families with good news.

She looked at him now, memories swimming in her heart.

"What?" Sam asked, as he noticed her persistent gaze.

"I was just thinking about…" She dropped her gaze. "Nothing. It was silly." There was no use going down a trail that she had blocked off.

"Nothing?" Sam asked, and stopped. Night had drawn a blanket over the sky and scattered stars overhead. Sam set the E-kit on the ground and placed his hands on Vicki's shoulders, turning her to face him. "With you, nothing is always something. What are you thinking about?"

Vicki shrugged, trying not to give in to the good memories of him, trying not to feel the strength in his hands, and trying to resist his body warming her in the cool night air. But finally she had to meet his gaze. "Of us. How we used to be. Part of me wants that again, but I don't think we can ever go back." Time always seemed against her, even now.

"No, we can't. We've both changed too

much to go back to what we used to be, even if we wanted to."

It was the absolute truth, and she'd demanded nothing less from him. They had both changed in ways they probably weren't even aware of. Tears sprang to her eyes, but she fought them, determined not to give in to the impulse to fling herself onto the ground and sob her heart out. She'd brought this on and she was now suffering the consequences.

"It's too late. I know."

CHAPTER FOURTEEN

OVER the next few days, Vicki and Sam barely had time to say hello to each other. Gil took Sam's suggestion and invited the insurance adjuster to the camp. While the administrator was busy going over policies, procedures, the books, and plans for improvement, Sam took over some of Gil's day-to-day chores, having little time in the infirmary other than to shower and drop into his cot for a few rough hours of sleep.

Vicki noted Sam's absence from the lodge during lunch one day. She hadn't been in there much herself lately. Since she'd started the tea over two weeks ago, her appetite wasn't what it had been. But nothing ever killed Sam's appetite, so where was he? Imagining he was too busy to take time to eat, she approached the cook.

"Hi, Bear. Could you make a tray for Sam? A couple of sandwiches and some coffee ought to do. I'll take it to him in the office." It was the least she could do. He was very busy, as was Gil, and she had more down time than they did at the moment.

"What? Can't the man take time to eat with the rest of us?" Bear asked, but pulled a tray from beneath the counter and began loading it up with more than enough food to see Sam through the next ice age.

"Uh, by the way, I love your clam chowder," Vicki said, and watched as Bear's large hands put together a beautiful presentation out of the simplest food.

"Best chowder in Maine," Bear said, and winked at Vicki, his small smile visible in the depths of his black beard streaked with gray.

"What's in it?" she asked, not daring to look directly at Bear and pretending interest in a stack of napkins.

"Clams, of course. Heavy cream, spices, a few other things," he said, his response vague as he put the finishing touches on the tray of food.

"I'd love to be able to make it this winter," Vicki said.

"Nurse Vicki," he chided, "you know I don't give out my recipes." Bear gave her a hard stare.

"Yes, I know. But you could save me from having to resort to *canned* clam chowder."

Bear grimaced as he handed the tray of food to Vicki. "Canned chowder?" Bear shuddered. "That's what's wrong in America these days.

Everybody wants instant food. Now, cooking from scratch is wholesome and full of healthy nutrients. There's not one preservative in *my* food," Bear claimed with a finger pointed at her. "Not one."

"That's why every meal you make is incredible," Vicki said. She was going to get that recipe out of Bear if it was the last thing she did before leaving camp.

With the tray of food in her hands, she carried it to Gil's office and found Sam sprawled asleep at Gil's desk. "Sam?" she called. "Wake up."

Sam didn't move, except to breathe.

Placing the tray to the side, Vicki touched Sam's shoulder and shook him. "Wake up, Sam. Chow time."

Sam finally stirred, stretched and opened his eyes. "Hi there."

"Were you up all night?" This was just like

the days when he had studied for board cer-tification. He'd pulled all-nighters, then, too.

"Yes. The insurance guy is driving Gil crazy, and Gil's driving me crazy. I feel like his personal secretary." Sam shrugged. "But it's OK, 'cos I think Gil's winning the guy over."

"That's good. I brought some food as you missed lunch."

Sam reached for a sandwich. "Is this all for me?"

"Yes, though Bear thought you should come to the lodge for meals like everyone else. I figured you forgot to eat, the way you used to in med school." Memories again swamped Vicki, and she cleared her throat to chase them away. "Well, I'll leave you to it."

"Wait. Don't go," Sam said, and reached out for her hand. "Why don't you share some of this? I can't possibly eat it all right now."

"No, but thanks. Since I started the herbal

tea my stomach hasn't been the same. The smell of food makes me nauseous. I'm mostly just drinking fluids and a few crackers now and then." Uck. Eat a plate of sandwiches now? No way.

Sam's gaze became instantly alert, though his voice was as soft as ever. "How long did you say you've had stomach trouble?"

"Since I started the tea. I didn't realize it was going to have this effect on me." Nausea wasn't listed among the side effects.

"Exactly when did you start the tea?"

"About two weeks ago, when…we… came…" Vicki dropped into a chair and clutched the seat. "I started it the day we came back from Fryeburg." Eyes wide, she started to hyperventilate. "Oh, no."

"After we made love." Sam stared at her, his expression unreadable.

No, she couldn't be pregnant. Not again.

Dear God, not again. Panic threatened to take over and stars appeared in her vision.

Sam reached out to touch her, but she pulled away. "Don't touch me. Every time you touch me I end up pregnant!" How did that happen? Why did that happen?

"Vicki, that's not true." He looked away. "Not *every* time."

She bolted up out of the chair and the stars spun in crazy circles, her vision narrowing to a small pinpoint. Then she was floating in the air, waiting to hit the floor.

Sam caught her before she dissolved into a puddle. "It's OK, baby, it's OK. I've got you." With her in his arms, he moved to the couch and laid her down. After a quick check of her pulse to reassure himself that it was just a faint, Sam got a washcloth, ran it under cool water and applied it to Vicki's forehead. While she rested, he splashed some water on his own face, thinking. Was now the time to approach her with the idea that had been brewing in his mind for weeks? Probably not, as she'd just fainted. One monumental item in a day was enough.

He returned to the couch and knelt beside her, watching her breathe. Guilt hammered in his head. This was where he should have been when she'd had the miscarriages—beside her, not at work. Here is where he should have been. Dammit! How could he not have seen how lost and alone she had been? He loved her and he'd left her alone.

Now his gaze ranged over her, from her face, tanned from the summer sun, down to her flat abdomen, moving gently with her respirations. Did a new life grow in there? Could their loving at the inn have been the start of more than one new life? That of a child and their own new life together? Could this be the answer he'd been waiting for?

He didn't know, couldn't guess. He wanted to revel in the possibilities. Unable to stop himself, he placed his hand on her belly, knowing he wouldn't feel anything but desperately wanting to connect. For the first time in a long time, wanting that life he and Vicki might have created to survive, thrive, and be their child. Now he just had to convince Vicki of it.

"Vick?" Sam touched her face with his trembling hand, smoothing her hair back. "Vicki? Can you wake up?"

"No. I don't want to," she whispered, and the pain in her voice rocked him. Tears emerged from beneath her lashes, and one by one he wiped them away.

"Wake up or it's smelling salts for you," he said. Her color had improved, and her pulse had become stronger.

"What are we going to do?"

"We'll get through this. I promise, we'll get through this. Together, if you'll let me." Sam cleared his throat. "Can you sit up now?"

Vicki opened his eyes and she removed the washcloth from her forehead. "I think so." She swung her legs over the edge of the couch and eased herself upright with Sam's hand at her back.

"First of all, we don't know that you're pregnant. Your symptoms could certainly be associated with the Candida tea. Shelby said you're going to go through a massive detox for several weeks. Since you've never taken it before, you don't know how your body's going to react to it."

"But what if—?"

"You'll drive us both crazy with the 'what-if' thing. Let's call Shelby about the tea and then get a pregnancy test." That was practical, wasn't it? Sam pulled out his cellphone and dialed.

But after a short conversation with Shelby, he was no closer to answering the question. "She said you could have some nausea with the tea, but it wasn't a common reaction." She'd actually said she'd never heard of nausea associated with the tea.

"See? I'm pregnant," she said, her attitude fatalistic.

"Let's be a little more scientific about this, shall we?" he asked. "When was your last period?"

"I don't know."

"You don't know? I thought you kept track of your cycles?"

"I haven't needed to keep track for months."

"OK. Well, the simplest thing would be a pregnancy test. Can you go to town to get one?" He didn't even know where they were kept in a store or pharmacy.

"No, clinic is about to start. Can you go?"

"No, Gil and I are meeting in a few minutes with the insurance guy. I'll try to get out of it as quickly as I can, but I have to be there for part of it."

Vicki stared at him. "Dammit, I need that test."

"Maybe I can call the pharmacy and ask them to deliver one."

"Oh, no. Call for an emergency pregnancy test? I'll never be able to walk into that pharmacy again." She stood and paced a few steps away, then turned back to him. "I'll ask Ginny to go for me. She has free time after dinner."

"Good idea. Call me as soon as she gets back with it."

"Why?"

"I'd like to be with you when you take the test." He stepped closer to her, but didn't touch her, his heart pounding so loud she could probably hear it. "Will you let me?"

Vicki searched his eyes, then nodded. "I'll call you," she said and left Sam staring after her.

Vicki made it through the short clinic without messing anything up. Her hands trembled, her stomach knotted, and she broke out in a cold sweat. As soon as the last child departed, she called Ginny and arranged for her to bring the test.

Pacing back and forth accomplished nothing. Charlie wanted to follow her across the room, mirroring her paces. "You must be part herding dog," she said, and knelt to ruffle his fur. "But you're just gonna make me crazy doing that." She opened the door and shooed him outside.

Ginny arrived moments later and hurried up the path to the infirmary. "I got it," she cried, holding up a brown paper bag, and looked around to see if anyone else was with them.

"Actually, I got two. I never believe the first one."

"Thanks, Ginny. You're a lifesaver," Vicki said, and took the bag from her as soon as she entered the room. In a few minutes she'd know either way.

Ginny enveloped Vicki in a tight hug. "It's going to be OK, no matter the outcome."

"I don't know that," Vicki said. "What if…?" She pulled back from Ginny with a sniff, not ready to be negative about it. "I need to call Sam. He wants to be here for the result."

"I'll call him," Ginny said, and picked up the phone. "You go pee in a cup."

Sam charged through the doors a few minutes later. "Vicki? Where are you?"

"Here," she said, as she emerged from the bathroom with the pregnancy test. "I'm ready if you are." Steeling her emotions, she couldn't look at either of them.

"Do you want me to stay or would you like some privacy?" Ginny asked.

"It's OK, you can stay," Vicki said. "You can help pick me up off the floor if it's positive."

"We've already had to do that once today," Sam reminded her. Though his voice reached out to her, his hands were shoved firmly in his pockets.

"Here goes," Vicki said, and dipped the stick into the cup of urine. "This is one of those any-time tests." Anxiety unfurled inside her as she watched the color zip across the little window. She checked the time. "In one minute, we'll know."

Sam and Ginny crowded on either side of her to watch the next change, and Vicki closed her eyes, her heart hammering in her throat. "I can't look. Tell me when it's over."

A few seconds later, Sam huffed out a sigh. "Well. There it is," he said.

"Yep," Ginny said.

"Well? What does it say?" Vicki asked, still afraid to open her eyes.

"I don't know whether you'll be disappointed, angry, excited, or what," Sam said, and placed a hand on her shoulder.

"What are you?" she asked.

"I'm...pleased."

And he was, she could hear it in his voice. The softness, the love, the warmth. She opened her eyes and looked.

Positive.

CHAPTER FIFTEEN

SHE cried. Not knowing whether to be happy, sad, angry, hopeful, or resigned, she cried out the frustration of the last pregnancies, the last months of deciding to leave Sam and now the pain of being pregnant again.

"It's not what you wanted to see, I know, but with all the things going on, there's a chance it could be a false positive," Sam said.

"I appreciate your optimism, but it's not. The literature says there's less than a one percent chance of it being wrong." Ginny brought her a glass of water and she took it, but didn't drink. "And my symptoms are there. My breasts are tender, but I thought it was because I was due for my period. And there's this unexplainable…heaviness in my uterus." Somehow, deep inside she'd known. Every time she'd known.

"Do you want to do the other test, just to verify?" Ginny asked.

"No. I'm sure it's right." She didn't need it. She had known since that afternoon. All the signs were there. It wasn't the tea, and nothing else was upsetting her stomach.

"You should check it first thing in the morning when your hormone levels will be at their highest, just to be sure. That's the most accurate." Sam cleared his throat, but continued to watch her.

"I know, thanks." Vicki sipped the water.

The screen door opened, and Gil walked in. "We did it!" The smile dropped from his face as he looked around the room. "Uh, is this a bad time?"

"I was just going," Ginny said. "Why don't you come with me?"

"OK," he said, and walked out with Ginny.

Vicki stared at Sam. "Our divorce is final in four weeks. Now what?"

"It doesn't have to be."

"What do you mean, it doesn't have to be? Nothing else has changed, except now I'm pregnant and don't want to be this time."

"Vicki, things have changed between us, you just don't want to see it and accept it."

"No, you're married to your job. That hasn't changed. Whether I'm pregnant or not, you'll *still* be married to your job. I'm not going through that any more." She shook her head. "I can't, Sam. Don't ask me. No matter how much I love you, I can't do it."

"You don't have to," Sam said, his voice soft,

and he held out a hand to her. "Will you sit down with me? There's something I want to talk to you about." Nerves like he'd never had surged through him. If she said no, he had no idea what he would do.

Heaving a troubled sigh, Vicki placed her hand in his. The warmth of his touch, even that simple, felt right. "How can this be so wrong?"

"It's not wrong. We are right together. I'm just damned sorry it's taken me so long to realize the sacrifice I had to make in my life shouldn't be my family." Admitting it to himself had been hard, admitting it out loud to Vicki was harder than anything he'd ever known. But for him to move on, to go on with her, he had to be honest with himself and with her. If there was the one thing he'd come away with, it was that he had to be honest about everything, no matter how painful it was.

"What?" Her breath stopped, and the beat of

her heart echoed in her ears. Staring at Sam, she could see the truth in his eyes. But she struggled to believe it. Not after all they'd been through, it just couldn't be that easy. "No. You may think that now, but when you get back to reality, when you get those calls at three in the morning, when you can't leave the hospital because of another critical case, it will all turn out the same. Nothing will have changed." She shook her head and looked away from him, unable to even think about how things could have been between them, not willing to think about what could have been.

Sam took her hands in his. "I need you to believe in me more now than ever. I have a plan, but without you it won't work and won't be worth it if you're not beside me."

"A plan?" Not very hopeful, she nodded for him to go on.

"Yes. One that I hope will work for all of us."

He placed his hand on her abdomen. "I want this to work for all of us."

"I'm not making promises, but tell me."

They sat on the swing. "Vicki, this is hard for me to admit, but I was wrong about so many things. I just couldn't see it. I was trying to protect you from my own grief when I should have shared it with you. Being a doctor doesn't make me right about everything."

"I could have told you that," she said with a slight smile.

"You did, but I didn't listen. If it's not too late, I'm listening now." He took a big breath and met her gaze. "I want to leave my job and move into adolescent psychiatry."

"But you love your job." Could he really make such a sacrifice for them? Would he? This was a complete surprise.

"I don't love it more than you. I'd quit

tomorrow, but we do have a mortgage to pay. This may take some time, because I'd have to return to residency for a while, but even the residency has much more normal hours than what I'm doing now." He smiled. "I feel very strongly that I can help kids and their families. The way I needed help after Derek's death and didn't get it." Sharing it out loud with Vicki made it more real than his imaginings.

Tears swimming in her eyes, she nodded. "You'd be a great psychiatrist, Sam. The kids would love you."

"Only if you're in this with me. I can't do it alone. I know that now, and I don't want to do it alone. I love you, Vick. That has never changed. We can start fresh, start new, and love each other like we did in the beginning."

"The other night you said we couldn't go back."

"We can't. We can go on, together, but with

the knowledge of how easily things can go wrong. If you'll have me. If you'll trust me again. If I can trust you again."

"Sam, this is so sudden, so overwhelming, I don't know what to think." Vicki placed her hands over her cheeks.

"I know. But the more I think about my career change, the more I know it's the right thing to do. I just don't want to do it without you." Never again.

She turned to him. "Just hold me for a little while, will you?" She needed his arms around her. "What am I going to do about the pregnancy? What if I lose this one, too?" Though she didn't want to think about it, she had to bring it out into the open. Losing this baby was a real possibility.

"You'll let me help take care of you. You'll take time off from work and rest. We'll monitor the Candidiasis on a regular basis.

This time around I want us to do things right from the very beginning."

"You're right." She paused. "But I've been as guilty as you. I've made things harder on you than they had to be, and I'm sorry. I do love you, Sam." She clutched him around the neck as the tears overflowed. "I love you."

Sobbing with relief in his arms, she gave up the past and chose to live in the present. "You'll never have to worry about me again."

"You'll never doubt me either." Sam kissed her, knowing that his life would only be complete with her beside him. Pulling back, he knelt in front of her. "Vicki, will you marry me, again?"

Nodding through her tears she said, "I will. I love you, Sam."

"I love you, too."

EPILOGUE

One year later, at Camp Wild Pines

GINNY burst through the door of the infirmary, a big smile on her face. "Where is she? Let me see her right now." She grabbed Vicki into a hug. "Oh, I can't wait to see her. Gimme, gimme, gimme."

Dancing up and down with Ginny, Vicki had to grin at her friend's enthusiasm. "She's asleep right now."

"Oh, darn!" Ginny said in an exaggerated whisper. "I wanted to see her the second I got here."

"Well, if you promise not to wake her, you can peek in on her."

"I promise, I promise."

Vicki took Ginny by the hand and led her to the room that used to be the ward room. She and Sam had rearranged the entire place so that the larger ward room would hold a bed for Vicki and Sam, as well as the crib for the baby. Ginny looked down at the sleeping infant wrapped snugly in her pink sleeper and covered with a fluffy quilt. "Oh, she's darling, just darling," Ginny whispered.

They left the room and returned to the main part of the infirmary. "I'm so happy for you," Ginny said. "She's just beautiful." She and Vicki sat at the little kitchen table. "So tell me how your year was. You look well, even though you have a three-month-old keeping you up nights."

"Thanks. This year couldn't have been better," Vicki said. "Sam and I were like kids again when we got home. We had a honeymoon all over again." Vicki blushed and looked away, but she couldn't keep the sparkle from her eyes. "And he kept every promise that he made. I quit my job and just concentrated on taking care of me during the pregnancy and now the baby." She laughed. "Sam was such a nervous father-to-be. You should have seen him."

"What did he do?" Ginny asked.

"He fussed over me every day, called me from work to make sure I was resting, bought organic everything and made a chart for tracking my weight. Not that I needed that. Drove me crazy sometimes, but really it was wonderful. More than I would have guessed possible at the end of last summer." Vicki paused and wiped her eyes. "We did everything as a team. I picked the color, and he painted the nursery. I chose the baby furniture, and he put it together. He was attentive, and loving, and everything I could have hoped for when we first married. I'm so glad that we were able to see things differently at the end of last summer. We've totally turned our marriage and our friendship around."

"No complications during the pregnancy?"

"Not one. I finished the treatment during the first trimester, took all the prenatal vitamins I needed to, and here we are. One happy, healthy, baby Myra."

"Myra. Is that a family name?"

"No, it actually means something like longed-for child."

"That's absolutely perfect," Ginny said. She reached out and hugged Vicki again, unable to contain her enthusiasm. "I'm thrilled for you and Sam. Of all of the couples I know, you two are the most solid, always have been."

"Oh, we have had our ups and downs, but

we've definitely been taking this time around more seriously, I think, than when we were first married. We've both grown individually and together, too."

The first tentative sounds of a baby cry had Ginny on her feet in a flash. "You stay here. I want to get her." She disappeared into the room and returned in a minute with the baby wrapped in her blanket.

"She's gorgeous, Vicki. Just gorgeous," Ginny said, and patted Myra's back.

"She's about due for a feed. When she gets cranky, she's not nearly as gorgeous then," Vicki said with a small laugh. "This has been a good year for us," she said, and took Myra from Ginny. "A very good year."

"After you feed her, can I hold her again?" Ginny asked.

"Sure. You just have to promise not to spoil her too much this summer. You'll set a precedent that I don't want to have to live up to the rest of her life."

"I promise," Ginny said, and watched as Myra cooed and settled down for her meal.

Sam entered the infirmary and kissed Vicki on the forehead. "How are you doing, Ginny?" he asked, and gave her a squeeze.

"Great, but nothing compared to you two. You look more in love than ever," she said. "I'm jealous."

Vicki and Sam looked at each other and smiled. "I guess we are. It took almost losing each other to realize that we were meant to be together," Sam said, and stroked a finger over Myra's cheek. "Contemplating divorce is a hell I don't ever want to go through again."

"Me neither," Vicki said.

"Tell me what's going on with your job, Sam."

"After we got back home last September, I cut back on my hours, delegated more responsibility, and applied for the psych residency. I start after camp this year."

"How will that work with having a baby at home?" Ginny asked, concern in her eyes.

"Fortunately, this residency is going to have much better hours than the surgical residency."

"And I'm going to be involved with a group of moms with new babies. By then Myra will be almost six months old, and I'll be ready for some adult company. That will keep us busy while Sam's at work."

"Sounds like you've got everything just about covered," Ginny said.

"I'm sure things will come up, but we're really working on communication."

"A little communication goes a long way," Ginny said. "I know firsthand."

Gil entered the infirmary just as Myra finished her feed, and Vicki handed her to Ginny. "Burping time."

"There's the little one," Gil said, and bent over to have a look at baby Myra sleeping on Ginny's shoulder. "Oh, she's beautiful. Just beautiful. Who do you think she looks like?"

"Sam."

"Vicki."

Vicki laughed and Sam pulled her into a hug. "We both think she looks like the other. But she'll probably turn out something completely different when she's done growing," Vicki said.

"Well," Gil said. "On to business. The kids get here tomorrow, most of the counselors are here and ready to go. Have you been able to walk around the camp yet?"

"I have, but Vicki hasn't," Sam said.

"After the fire last year, we've finally finished the soccer field. This spring some of the cabins got new roofs, thanks to that insurance man." Gil rubbed his hands together. "Great idea, Sam."

"When Myra is awake again, we'll take a walk out and see the changes. We basically pulled the van up to the front door, unloaded, and here we are."

"Van? What happened to the Mustang?" Gil asked. "I thought you loved that car."

"I did, but I love Sam more," Vicki said, and looked at her husband. "We traded the Mustang for a family van."

"When Myra's grown, you can have another hotrod, Vick."

"Thanks," she said with a grin, and then chewed her lower lip. "Should I ask him now?"

"Why not? He's in a good mood. Go ahead," Sam said.

"What are you talking about?" Gil asked, looking back and forth between them.

"We were wondering if we could have a party here. It's been such a whirlwind of a year for both of us that we haven't had time for much of a breather until now."

"What kind of party are you talking about?" Gil asked, and took a seat at the table.

"We wanted to renew our vows here." Vicki watched him for a reaction. "Because this place, and you, were instrumental in helping us get back together."

"Me? What did I do?"

"You nagged me and made me feel guilty until I agreed to come for the summer," Vicki said with a laugh.

"Nag? I never nag," Gil said.

"No matter how you look at it, you were the reason I came back to camp last year. We want to renew our vows and have a party in celebration of this little family. Our extended family at camp is very important to us, and we wanted to include them and the kids in the party."

"Wow. That sounds like a great idea! The

kids will love it. Just let me know what you need from me, and I'll be happy to do it."

"How is the other nurse, by the way?" Sam asked, and stroked Vicki's hair as they talked. "She recovered fully from her accident?"

"Yes. You'll get to meet her pretty soon. She's going to be here to take over some of Vicki's duties as we have baby Myra this year."

"Oh, great." Tears pricked Vicki's eyes. "I hadn't expected the extra help." She reached out and kissed Gil on the cheek. "Thank you."

"You are very welcome. I'm just glad everything turned out for the best. Now, tell me when you want the party."

Several weeks later the day of the planned party arrived. Ginny adjusted the flowers in Vicki's hair. "You look beautiful," she said. "Just beautiful. And so is your little bridesmaid." Ginny touched Myra's pink headband.

"I'm so glad we're renewing our vows here. This is so much more fun than our first wedding." Vicki laughed and thought back to that time. "Sam was so nervous back then, he threw up before the ceremony."

Ginny clucked her tongue. "Poor guy. I think he's in better shape this time. Just look at him."

Sam waited for them at the dock. He wore tan shorts, a brightly colored Hawaiian shirt and sandals on his feet.

"Better than formal wear any day," Vicki said, and adjusted the straps of her sundress. Though they wore casual clothing, their commitment to each other was anything but. This time their commitment seemed more dear, more real than the first time, especially with baby Myra in their lives. They had more to keep them together than they'd ever had.

Gil arrived at the infirmary. "I'm here to escort the bride to her groom."

"Thank you, Gil." Vicki kissed his cheek. "I'm ready."

"I'll take Myra now, and we'll go first," Ginny said.

As they walked outside into the bright sunshine, Vicki donned her sunglasses and took Gil's arm. "Here we go," she said. Beach music played over the intercom and the camp had the festive air of a beach party.

With two hundred kids and counselors as witnesses, Sam and Vicki recommitted themselves to each other. Then Sam kissed Vicki and pulled her into his embrace. "Where's my other girl?" he asked, and motioned Ginny forward.

"There she is. This isn't a party until I have both my girls in my arms." Sam took Myra from Ginny and held her to his chest. "You two are my family, and I will never forget it," he said.

Tears swam in Vicki's eyes, and she blinked them away, wanting Sam to see the commitment in her eyes. "Neither will I." She kissed Sam again and the party began.

Later, Bear approached Vicki as she was about to settle into a chair to feed Myra. "Hi, Bear. This is a great party. Thank you so much for making it happen for us."

"You're welcome. My pleasure to help out." He adjusted his hat and looked down at the envelope in his hand. "I almost forgot to give this to you." He handed a plain white envelope to her.

"What's this? After all this, I can't accept any presents from you, Bear. You've already done too much for us."

"Well, it's just a little thing, but I expect you can use it come winter." He bent over and looked at the baby. "She's a beaut," he said, then stood upright again. "I gotta go make sure they don't burn the place down like last year."

"Bye, Bear," Vicki said, as she looked at the

envelope. "Use it come winter, eh?" she said aloud, and tore open the envelope.

She laughed and clasped the white card inside to her chest. "Thank you, Bear," she yelled. Though he didn't turn, he raised his arm in acknowledgment.

"What do you have there?" Sam asked as he romped around with Jimmy on his back.

"Bear gave me his recipe for clam chowder! I can't believe it," she said.

"Wow," Sam said, and swung Jimmy round and placed him on the ground. "He's never done that before."

"Can I see your baby?" Jimmy asked, his eyes wide as he approached.

"Sure you can," she said. "But first you have to give me a hug. I haven't seen you in a year, and you're so much taller," she said, and held out an arm. Jimmy squeezed her tight and then pulled back.

"I'm with a family I like now," he said voluntarily. Gone was the shy, fearful little boy of last year. He had grown in more than height.

"I'm so happy you have a good place and a good family now," Vicki said, and kissed him on the cheek.

"Yeah, my new mom is going to have a baby, too. I've never seen one up close," he said with a shrug, but never took his eyes from Myra. "She's really small."

"She is just the right size for her age. When she's done feeding you can hold her if you like." Vicki hoped that he would take to having a little brother or sister well.

"Really? Cool." Jimmy looked around. "Where's Charlie?"

"He's here somewhere," Sam said. "I imagine he's getting reacquainted with everyone."

"I'm gonna go look for him. I hope he remembers me," Jimmy said, and raced off.

"Jimmy has really done well this year," Vicki said, and turned Myra over for a burping.

"Gil told me the state found a wonderful family who has adopted several children."

"Sam? Vicki?" Gil approached. "I'm sorry I can't let you have time off for a proper second honeymoon, but we obviously need you both in camp right now."

"It's OK. We'll be fine," Sam said.

"What I can offer you is use of the administrative house for two weeks after the kids leave at the end of summer, before you have to head off to your residency. You can stay there, tour New England, relax, and enjoy your time together as a family. The camp won't be locked down for the winter yet, so it's yours to use."

"Oh, thank you, Gil." Vicki hugged him. "You've done so much for us."

"My pleasure to see you happy together."

Sam looked at Vicki and baby Myra. "We're happy to be together. More than you can possibly know."

MEDICAL™

Large Print

Titles for the next six months…

October

THE DOCTOR'S ROYAL LOVE-CHILD — Kate Hardy
HIS ISLAND BRIDE — Marion Lennox
A CONSULTANT BEYOND COMPARE — Joanna Neil
THE SURGEON BOSS'S BRIDE — Melanie Milburne
A WIFE WORTH WAITING FOR — Maggie Kingsley
DESERT PRINCE, EXPECTANT MOTHER — Olivia Gates

November

NURSE BRIDE, BAYSIDE WEDDING — Gill Sanderson
BILLIONAIRE DOCTOR, ORDINARY NURSE — Carol Marinelli
THE SHEIKH SURGEON'S BABY — Meredith Webber
THE OUTBACK DOCTOR'S SURPRISE BRIDE — Amy Andrews
A WEDDING AT LIMESTONE COAST — Lucy Clark
THE DOCTOR'S MEANT-TO-BE MARRIAGE — Janice Lynn

December

SINGLE DAD SEEKS A WIFE — Melanie Milburne
HER FOUR-YEAR BABY SECRET — Alison Roberts
COUNTRY DOCTOR, SPRING BRIDE — Abigail Gordon
MARRYING THE RUNAWAY BRIDE — Jennifer Taylor
THE MIDWIFE'S BABY — Fiona McArthur
THE FATHERHOOD MIRACLE — Margaret Barker

MILLS & BOON®
Pure reading pleasure™

0908 LP 2P P1 Medical

MEDICAL™

Large Print

January

February

March

MILLS & BOON®

Pure reading pleasure™

0908 LP 2P P2 Medical